Death and the Remembrancer

Accidents on grouse moors are not uncommon, but the violent death of a gamekeeper whose dissolute ways have caused distress in a Highland village is a matter which concerns both the police and Edward Williams, the local minister. Others seem less concerned.

Life in a village is always more complex than it appears and it can take a long time before an incomer (even, or especially, the minister or the police) is allowed to know the currents which lie beneath the surface, and in the memories of the inhabitants. Past errors are not forgotten, and have their consequences.

How the gamekeeper had died was only too clear. Between them, Williams and his friend Superintendent Mason come to think they know who shot him, and why.

FRANCIS LYALL

Death and the Remembrancer

COLLINS, 8 GRAFTON STREET, LONDON W1

William Collins Sons & Co. Ltd
London · Glasgow · Sydney · Auckland
Toronto · Johannesburg

First published 1988
© Francis Lyall 1988

British Library Cataloguing in Publication Data

Lyall, Francis
    Death and the remembrancer.—(Crime Club)
    I. Title
    823'.914[F]   PR6062.Y2/

ISBN 0 00 232169 6

Photoset in Linotron Baskerville by
Rowland Phototypesetting Ltd
Bury St Edmunds, Suffolk
Printed in Great Britain by
William Collins Sons & Co. Ltd, Glasgow

ONE: AUGUST

1

'It was a beautiful funeral,' Miss Andrews confided to her friend in the late afternoon. 'Poor Mr Williams. It must be so difficult to say something suitable when you know absolutely nothing about the deceased. But it was so beautiful.'

'He knew who he was,' said Mrs Jenkins. 'He was Mildred Anthony's nephew.'

'Yes, I know. But no one knew anything about him until —was it in the spring? Everyone thought Mildred had no relatives. And he had only been here less than a month.'

'Yes. I suppose so,' said Mrs Jenkins wearily. She knew better than to argue with her friend once she had an idea into her head.

'But Mr Williams conducted a beautiful service. Beautiful,' said Miss Andrews decisively, sitting back in her chair.

'But I thought . . .' began Mrs Jenkins.

'No contradiction,' said Miss Andrews, with the speed of a retired teacher. 'It was a beautiful service, but not pleasant. It was so cold in the graveyard.'

'Oh, you went out to the interment as well.' Mrs Jenkins was clearly surprised.

'I know,' replied Miss Andrews with an apologetic cough. 'But there were so few there. I felt that I had to. It didn't seem right to wait on in the church. And in any event I'm told that in Greyhavens it is the custom that everyone goes to the graveyard nowadays. Even the ladies.'

Mrs Jenkins nodded, her face expressionless.

'But you were wise not to have come,' went on her friend. 'The wind seemed to be coming straight from the Arctic. I was glad I had on my heavy coat.'

Mrs Jenkins coughed politely.

'There you are, said Miss Andrews. 'You would have caught your death of cold.'

'Speaking of which,' said Mrs Jenkins, raising her head to peer at the clock, 'I have Mr Wade coming soon. We have things to discuss.'

'Not your will again,' said Miss Andrews as both got to their feet and crossed to the door. There, as was their custom, they stopped and looked out of the window down at the elegant tree-lined drive.

'I am afraid so,' said Mrs Jenkins. 'I am afraid that I have not been quite just in the way I have treated my brother's stepchildren. I think that after all they should get something. I had a letter the other day from Michael, the youngest. He seems to be a nice boy. So polite.'

'Ah,' said Miss Andrews archly. Then, realizing that she might have overstepped a mark as Mrs Jenkins frowned, she added, 'But you have never seen any of them, and you told me your brother did leave them comfortable.'

'I know. I know,' said Mrs Jenkins testily. 'But I was lying in bed the other night, sleepless as usual, and it came to me that it would be a nice gesture to remember them. Not much. Just a token. Perhaps five hundred.'

'Each?' said Miss Andrews.

At that point there was the sound of tyres on gravel, and a large white car drew to a halt on the drive. A man in a dark suit got out. He waved as he caught sight of the two figures at the window.

'He wasn't at the funeral,' observed Miss Andrews.

'Well, after all . . .' said Mrs Jenkins faintly.

'Yes. I suppose so,' said Miss Andrews. 'Well, Margaret, I had better be going.'

As Wade walked across the gravel Mrs Jenkins sighed.

'His father was such a nice man,' she said.

'So they say,' said Miss Andrews.

'I forgot. You never knew Mr Wade did you?'

'No. He died some years before I moved to the village. But they say the son slipped into his shoes quite effortlessly.'

As they moved down the stairs Mrs Jenkins continued, 'Yes. It was good that he came back to the old home. It is such a beautiful house, and full of such treasures. It would have been a pity if it had been sold.'

Miss Andrews pursed her lips.

'I meant the practice,' she said. 'Still, the house will have to be sold in due course if he doesn't get a move on and get married soon. He must be quite into his forties by now.'

At the foot of the stairs Miss Andrews paused to adjust her coat. Mrs Jenkins opened the front door.

Wade entered. 'I'm not interrupting am I?' he said with a smile.

'No. Not at all. I was just leaving,' replied Miss Andrews.

Mrs Jenkins bade her goodbye, and as she closed the door, Miss Andrews heard her say to Peter Wade, 'I am sorry to have had to call you in once more, but . . .'

At the corner of the drive, Miss Andrews glanced back at the old house, but there was now no one at the creeper-lined lounge window.

She smiled to herself. Sorry indeed! Mrs J., as she always thought of her friend, had been changing her will for years. Indeed, there were times when getting her inheritance properly divided among her numerous relatives seemed to be the main purpose in her life. Pity that there was never any mention of something for her friends. Briefly she wondered if Wade got a fee for every change in the list of beneficiaries. Certainly he seemed attentive enough. But when she herself had asked him a civil question—in the abstract, of course —he had shrugged it aside. Oh well, a retired schoolteacher did not have the capital of a banker's widow.

She tossed her head slightly, and thought of other things.

Such a pity about Mildred Anthony's nephew. She must call again to offer her condolences. Mildred had not seemed to have understood what she was saying the last time she had visited. But then her grasp of things did seem to come and go. Age! Miss Andrews pursed her lips again, and her walk firmed up. Age indeed!

2

The Rev. Edward Williams had seen the funeral differently. Round about the time Miss Andrews was taking her leave of Mrs Jenkins, he sat, leaning forward over a coal fire, his hands cupped round a mug of tea his wife had just brought to him.

'It was pretty awful,' he said moodily.

His wife sat on the arm of his chair and ran her fingers through his hair.

'I know,' she said softly. 'I was thinking of you.'

'Why do people insist on a religious funeral, when it is quite obvious that the deceased had no interest in God or any sort of spiritual matters?' he said peevishly.

'You *are* the parish minister,' she replied.

'It's primitive,' he went on. 'As though the minister was some sort of medicine man, who could fix things with the gods.'

'But a funeral is more for the benefit of the mourners than the dead. That's what you always say.'

'I suppose so. But it's so false to go through our traditional burial service when you have no idea what is going to happen to the man in eternity.'

'He did come to church,' she ventured.

'Once. And then only because his aunt had told him to come.'

'Did she?' She chuckled, breaking the tension, and he

responded, 'Well, that's the way he put it to me. He actually said to me at the door, "My aunt said it was my duty."' Williams leaned back, smiling at the recollection. 'She must have been talking to him of the responsibilities which would soon be his.' The last few words were said ponderously. 'Still, that's all over now.' His mood changed.

A quietness stole into the room. The two sat and watched the firelight.

Eventually she broke the silence.

'He wasn't there, was he?'

'Who?'

'Peter.'

'No. You didn't expect him to be, did you?'

'Not really. But he is the Clerk.'

'That would really have fixed it. There were a couple of reporters there at the back. I can just see what some of the papers might have made of it. "Killer attends funeral."'

'They couldn't do that, could they? There's been no charge.'

'No. I suppose they couldn't have put it quite like that. But if he had been there, I couldn't very well have said that Peter was sorry for the accident.'

'Nor could you explain to reporters that he is such a punctilious man that as one of the senior office-bearers in the church he would feel it his duty to be there irrespective of his personal feelings.'

Williams smiled.

'Annie, Annie. He is a pain with his precision and that burden of duties. But he wasn't there, and I was grateful. His "duty" must have given way to sense at last.'

His face tightened again. 'But it was awful to stand at yet another graveside, and say the words of committal with no real hope. I almost felt like twisting them. You could change "in the sure and certain hope of the Resurrection" to "in,

I'm sure, the uncertain hope of the Resurrection". No one would notice if you slurred the words a bit, and it would be more accurate.'

'Well, that's wrong for a start,' said Ann Williams briskly as she got to her feet. 'Everyone will be resurrected. It's after that the uncertainties come in with Judgement Day. But I must go and get the tea started. The kids will be home soon, and remember that the Masons are coming. What would you like?'

Williams got to his feet. 'I'm sure you've got everything well arranged already,' he said. 'I'm going up to see that everything is all right up at Williamston.'

'Well,' she replied with a grin, 'in your absence I have been conducting crash trials. There was a new advert on the tele that gave me some ideas.'

He growled at her as she escaped from the room.

He made his way up to the attic room and his beloved model railway.

3

Later that evening Williams and Mason were ensconced in the attic, playing trains. Paul, Williams's son, had been spoken to before the Masons had arrived, and so did not attempt to follow his father and his friend as they got up and left the fireside.

'You've done a lot since I was here last,' said Mason, looking round appreciatively.

'Not really,' replied Edwards. 'It was just at that stage, and Duncan Raeburn was in on Monday afternoon. He helped me with the station.'

Mason bent over to look more carefully at the station in the corner.

'Beautiful. Beautiful,' he breathed.

'Look,' said Williams, handing him a small dentist's mirror.

With the instrument Mason checked various aspects of the Square in front of the station. The clock showed the same time on its concealed face as it did on the one visible from Mason's vantage point. The back side of the advertising hoarding box being pulled by the old gentleman exhorted the viewer to prepare to meet his God, just in case he had failed to take in the message about the forthcoming end of the world on the front of the box. Neither message seemed to make any difference to the girl who was clearly tearful as she said farewell to the strapping soldier at the entrance to the station. Across the road a bus was disgorging passengers, while a military lorry was off-loading other ranks inside the station yard.

'You have done a power of work up here,' said Mason, straightening up and looking round. He paced along beside the trestles, looking at this and that. Behind him Williams beamed, modestly, of course.

'Well, I told you that I was determined to stick to my timetable,' he said. 'I could have done with you last week. Can't a senior police officer arrange his life to suit himself?'

Mason shrugged. 'Catch me telling the court that I was very sorry but the trial would have to be postponed because I had to help build a railway?' He chuckled.

Williams laughed as well. 'You might have managed if it had been old Tooter. He's a member of the East British Railway Study Group.'

'Is he?' said Mason. 'Never.'

'He is. He is. I was talking to Hector, their Secretary, at the recent exhibition in Newcastle. We were talking about how widespread the membership of the railway societies is, and he said he had everything from unemployed tool-fitters from Glasgow to a High Court judge,' replied Williams. 'I noticed in the paper that it was that judge that was up for the trial. Still, I dare say he would see his duty to lie in a different direction.' He looked solemn, delivering the last sentence.

Mason laughed again, and then settled. 'Yes, he would do his duty. But he's a fine judge. Didn't let either side away with anything.'

'Is it true that there has never been a successful appeal from any trial he's taken?'

'So I believe,' said Mason, picking up an engine to examine it. 'I say, you've finished Glen Mamie.'

'Yes,' said Edwards. 'Want to see her run?'

'Please.'

But it wasn't as easy as that. There proved to be a cracked power rail in the layout at the part where the track went behind the chimney embrasure, and it took some time first to find the offending rail, and then to replace it. Once things were fixed, however, everything went smoothly.

'I still think,' said Mason, 'you've complicated the shunting area unnecessarily. It's an anachronism.'

'Not at all,' said Williams. 'There was a recent article in *The Shunter* which showed how complicated the sidings were east of Waverley so as to make maximum use of the space available. That was 1914, just like this.'

'Oh, all right, all right,' said Mason. 'I should know better than to challenge you on a matter like that.'

Williams smiled, got up and went to the other side of the attic, away from the controllers.

He fiddled with a box sitting at the side and put something, which Mason could not see, on the track. 'Try that on number three,' he said.

Mason powered up, and then started laughing as into view came a very modern '125' engine.

'I was nearly down here a week ago,' he said conversationally as he drew the engine to a halt beside the controller so that he could look at it more closely.

'The shooting?'

'Yes.'

'Sad business. I had the funeral this afternoon, early on.'

'Yes. I knew that. Gilchrist told me.'

Mason picked up the engine. 'You've got the lights working?'

'Yes. It was pretty awkward to lead the wiring through some of the holes, and I broke a few, but fine tweezers was the solution.'

Mason bent to put the engine back on the track. As he concentrated apparently on what he was doing, he said almost dreamily, 'Gilchrist wasn't entirely happy, you know.'

'How do you mean?' said Williams, surprised.

Mason straightened, and, turning the controller, sent the engine on its way into the tunnel behind the chimneystack.

'I don't really know,' he replied. 'It was just something he said to me.' He watched the train come out on the other side of the attic.

'It's probably nothing, but he just passed a comment. Something like, "Lucky you, having the court."'

'And?' said Williams.

'And I said, "I could have done with a few hours out in the fresh air rather than that." And he said that it was a bit weird.'

'Weird?'

'I don't know what he meant. But I think he found Wade difficult.'

Williams shook his head.

'Doesn't everyone?' he asked.

'I know,' said Mason. 'He is an odd bloke. We come across him infrequently. He stopped doing criminal work about six–seven years ago. Has a better sort of client, I suppose, now that he's back in among his father's practice. But when you do meet him professionally, you wonder whether there is anyone there behind his eyes. And if there is what he is thinking.'

Williams nodded. 'I know what you mean,' he said. 'I remember Ann saying she reckoned that he was radio-controlled, and I said, if so, it was by someone on the Moon. There always seems to be a delayed response.'

Mason laughed.

'But that couldn't be the answer,' Williams went on. 'He has excellent reflexes. I remember he was one of the three of us from the Kirk Session that went to inspect the Boys' Brigade last year. It was during their table-tennis competition night as it happened, and the Captain challenged any one of us to take on the winner. Wade did and won. I think it was twenty-one seven. Marvellous stuff. And he is an able organist. If you ever heard him playing the organ, even the old thing we have here, you would wonder. And I have heard him in the Cathedral. I've even found myself wishing Miss Hopkins would give up, but I know he would never take on the organ as a regular thing.'

'No?'

'No.'

'Even if you asked?'

'Even if I asked. He would think that it is not for the Session Clerk to play the organ.'

'What about the fiddle?' asked Mason wryly.

Williams smiled. 'Don't you folk know anything about the law of defamation?'

''Course not,' said Mason stoutly. 'That's civil law.'

He moved, and joggled the controller. The 125 screamed down the straight, and came to grief at the level-crossing in the far-away corner.

'Flaming amateurs,' said Williams, moving round to clear things up.

4

Next morning, Williams stretched as he came out of the study.

'That you?' came Ann's voice.

'Yes,' he called. 'Any chance of coffee?'

'I'll put the kettle on,' she replied. 'You'd better check the answer-phone. There were at least two calls came in while you were working in the garden. Did you check them?'

He came into the kitchen and put his arms round her as she filled the kettle.

'Not yet,' he said. 'I said I'd check the box again at eleven, and it's only half past ten.'

She wriggled free and crossed to the kettle lead and plugged it in.

'Not going too well?' she asked, concerned.

He shook his head. 'No,' he said. 'I can't get past that funeral yesterday. Whatever I start to write, the bleakness of the thing keeps coming back. Those few folk in the cold wind. All of them there for formality's sake, not for the poor fellow himself.'

'But that's what happens,' she replied. 'You said how grim a hopeless funeral is.'

'This was a peak, I hope.'

'But you've done your part.'

'I suppose that's part of it. It was very much a part. I had no sympathy with him . . . or with them. I was just the shaman going through the appropriate motions.'

She frowned. 'I'm sure you weren't doing that.'

He shrugged.

'Did I tell you that Evan Hughes was there?' he asked.

'Was he?'

He grinned. 'No, he wasn't,' he said.

'But you just said . . .' Then she saw the grin, and laughed in response. 'Oh, you!'

The kettle started to bubble.

She was serious again. 'That's good,' she said. 'He's never shown any interest.'

'No,' said Williams, moving over to look out of the window. 'All he has ever been willing to talk about has been the countryside and wildlife, and how badly he is paid by the PenIron Estate.'

'Why does he stay?'

'I don't know. Everyone says he is an excellent ghillie if you are out with him, and a good gamekeeper. They say he has greatly increased the number of birds on the estate, and has almost got the deer to the stage that they are farming them. I imagine he could get a job anywhere. He's good.'

'But there is his other reputation?' said Ann wryly.

'Oh, you've heard about that.'

'Can't do anything else. If you are talking to any of the mothers when he comes down the street, they'll make some comment.'

'Oh, *that* reputation. I thought you meant the drink.'

'That too,' said Ann.

The kettle clicked itself off. She picked up the teapot and turned to fill it. He came close and put his hand over hers.

'Coffee, woman. Coffee!' he said.

'What have you been hearing about Hughes?' asked Williams as they settled down with their coffees in the lounge.

'Nothing specific,' she said. 'But he does seem to have a reputation as a ladies' man. I mean, no one in the village now has actually been named to me as one of his conquests, but there is one story and all sorts of dark hints about him.'

'Such as?'

'Well, I gather that one family emigrated a couple of

years ago, just before we arrived, to split up a romance between him and their eldest daughter.'

'Not really. That's rather extreme.'

'Well, it is and it isn't. I wouldn't care to predict how you might react if, say, Jenny took up with someone like Evan Hughes when she is sixteen or so.'

'Is that what happened?'

'Apparently. There was a fourteen-year-old, mature for her years, physically at least, who had taken up with him. When she was found out, she apparently told her parents that as soon as she was sixteen she was going to move in with Hughes. So they upped and moved to north of Brisbane, it seems. Father was an accountant, I believe.'

'You mean the Craigs? The one who was the Clerk to the Board before Isaac Watson? He went to Australia.'

Ann nodded, cupping her hands round her coffee mug, and leaning forward earnestly. 'I didn't know that,' she said. 'But if it fits it would be them, I suppose.'

'Well, they did move to Australia in some haste. Ian Paterson over at Linxton told me that. I had been hunting for something which should have been in the Clerk's files, but Isaac couldn't produce it, and Peter didn't have a copy, surprisingly. I didn't press Isaac because I knew he took the job on only recently, and wasn't going to keep it either. But Ian and I were coming back from Presbytery some time last year and I mentioned it. The Presbytery had been discussing a report on readjusting parishes and I could have done with seeing a previous report. I was saying that if I had got my hands on that I might have managed to mince the Convener of the Ad Hoc Committee. But the Craigs' going had left everything in a mess. Ian said that the Craigs had sold up and left within three months. And you know there are rumours in the village still about that. Some think he decamped with the funds of his firm.'

'Sometimes I think the church will drown itself in bits of paper,' said Ann.

'No doubt. But at least it is not as complicated as dealing with human beings. Sometimes I think some of my ministerial colleagues retreat into committees just like barons used to withdraw into castles when the world outside got too hot for them.'

'You do too,' she said.

'Do I?'

'Sometimes.'

'Well, not always. Here we are discussing parish matters.'

'Black sheep.'

'Goats, even.'

'He is a bit of a goat,' she said reflectively.

'Well, that is his reputation, though I didn't know the Craig bit.'

'The minister rarely knows much, and his wife less,' she replied.

'I'm glad you told me,' said Williams. 'But I wish you had told me earlier. It makes some sense of odd things Hughes has said when I was visiting.'

'It is also rumoured that there's been at least one abortion in the last year or so, attributable to him. Not to add certain marriages under strain both here in the village and over in Linxton.'

Williams smiled. 'The benefits of a pedal cycle,' he said.

She smiled in reply, and then went serious again.

'I'm not sure what we can do about it.'

'I don't think we have anything to do. It's a few centuries since the minister could name a parish offender from the pulpit. And in any event there would have to be a trial by the Kirk Session.'

She laughed. 'What a wonderful thought. I dare say that Peter Wade might do it very well.'

'Yes,' he replied. 'Apparently, before he became as respectable as he is nowadays, Wade figured in a lot of criminal trials.'

'Citizen's defender?'

'Sort of. There was a system of poor law representation. Young lawyers would do a month at a time as a sort of duty solicitor in the courts for anyone who couldn't afford a lawyer. It helped in getting experience, and in getting over court room nerves. But also certain firms and certain people would put their names down for that sort of work to make a living while waiting to get their names known to a better class of client. Then, once they were established, they could do without that work.'

'That sounds horrible,' Ann said. 'Get on your feet and kick away the ladder that got you up. I don't like lawyers.'

'Oh, they're not all like that. And it is true that anyone will defend anyone if they are nobbled to do it. Some see it as a social duty to keep on doing that sort of job, to a limited extent at least. But the fact does remain that there were some who used and maybe still use it as their own form of social security payment. Still, the point is that that is how Wade got his start.'

She giggled. 'He's put that a long way behind him, hasn't he?'

'Yes. He must have been lucky to have inherited that fat practice from his father. But still I find myself sometimes wondering whether he has gained the whole world.' He shrugged, spreading his hands as he did so.

'And lost . . .' Her voice trailed off. She drained her coffee briskly, and got up.

'I'll send you back to work,' she said. 'Start again, and I'm sure something will come.'

Williams finished his coffee with one swig and handed her the mug. 'Only one way to see,' he said.

She stopped, still holding the mug out towards him, and then slowly drew it back.

'I've just realized what you said,' she said slowly.

'What? Which?'

'About Hughes.'

'What about Hughes?'

'That he was there at the funeral.'

'Yes. What about it.'

'Is that hopeful?'

'I don't know. It seems he was acting as Wade's loader, and was in the butt when the accident happened.'

'The accident may have got through to him.'

'Maybe. We'll have to wait and see, won't we.' He gave her a gentle shove towards the door.

She gave her head a shake, clearing as it were, with a theatrical gesture.

'Better check the black box, and then you can write a blistering sermon about village morals and sudden death,' she said as she went out of the room.

'Hardly,' he said to her retreating back. 'Just think what it would be like to have something like that in the sermon, and then to see his nose poking at you from the gallery.'

She turned, laughing. 'I could just see you throwing your script into the air, and having a sudden attack of laryngitis, if that happened,' she said. 'No courage.'

He stuck his elbows out and flapped them. 'Prrraw. Tuck, tuck, tuck,' he said.

'You're no chicken,' she threw back over her shoulder as she went along the passage.

Two minutes later he came back into the kitchen with an odd smile on his face.

'Come, listen to this,' he said.

She followed him through to the study. He picked up the telephone and handed it to her. Then he switched the answer-phone to 'play'.

The first message was a request to phone Ian Paterson over in Linxton to confirm the golf date they had, if there was one. Paterson was not sure.

The second was abrupt.

'Hughes here. If you want to try stalking, come to my place tomorrow morning before eight. Bring a packed lunch.'

'Well?' asked Ann, handing back the receiver.

'Corned beef, I think,' he said. 'And a couple of lettuce and tomato.'

She hit him. Hard.

5

'How has she been today?' asked Williams, as he followed the nurse upstairs.

'Not too bad, really. Of course, she has still not got over the death of her nephew.'

'Yes, I know. It was a great shock. To have had an heir and then to have lost him all so suddenly. A great tragedy.'

The nurse turned at the top of the stairs to lead him along the corridor, but then glanced at him.

'There can't be a God if such things happen,' she said, with pursed lips.

'Yes, there is,' he said. 'If there is no God then the whole thing is meaningless.'

She looked at him piercingly, and then moved on.

'This way,' she said.

Miss Winifred Mildred Anthony lay propped up on pillows in the middle of a large bed. As Williams entered she appeared to flourish something, and then laid down the remote controller for the television which sat on a cantilever table at the end of the bed.

'I hope I am not interrupting something,' he said.

'Not at all. Not at all, Minister,' she said. 'I must confess a certain weakness for these soap operas as they seem to call them nowadays, but I am not yet an addict. Perish the thought that I would prefer television to human company.'

Williams smiled, and drew up the seat which sat at the side of the bed.

'How are you today?' he said.

'So-so,' she replied.

He frowned. He had never known this doughty old woman to be anything less than honest—bitterly honest, some would say. Her beaky nose lifted. Age accentuated its impact. He found himself wondering if there were a family connection with the Sitwells for certainly she reminded him strongly of the older Edith Sitwell.

'It has been a great shock,' she said, her fingers playing together. 'First, I thought my brother was the end of our line. Then, this personable young man appears, clearly an Anthony. I reconciled myself to that—I had to—and then . . .'

Williams leaned forward and patted the twisting hands.

'You mustn't distress yourself,' he said awkwardly.

It was the wrong thing to say. The old woman pulled herself straighter in her bed and firmly clasped her hands together.

'I must thank you for the dignity with which you conducted the funeral,' she said. 'I have heard several reports. It must have been difficult as we knew Harold for such a short time.'

'He made a deep impression even in a few weeks,' returned Williams. 'And in any event a funeral is a solemn occasion.'

'Weddings and funerals. Weddings and funerals,' she said, settling down again against the pillows. 'That is what they say life consists of in a small village like ours.'

'And baptisms,' ventured Williams.

She snorted. It sounded to Williams suspiciously close to a constricted laugh. 'Not always in that order,' she said.

He was silent.

'In the old days,' she explained, 'the village was fairly notorious round about for the number of weddings that were followed by baptisms within the statutory period.'

'It must have made things difficult for my predecessors,' he said with a slight smile.

'Indeed,' she said. 'Why, I can remember . . .' The voice trailed off, and the expression softened.

'Is there anything I can do?' he asked at last.

She dragged her attention back to the present.

'There is little that anyone can do for an old woman who has lived beyond her time,' she said. 'But a minister can at least pray for her.'

Williams found himself blushing.

She leaned forward and patted his hand.

'That was unfair of me,' she said. 'I have heard of the good work that you are doing. Mrs Jenkins has been bringing me the recordings of your sermons for some time.'

'I didn't know that,' he said.

'I found them difficult. But there was something you said quite early on in one of the first that caught my attention. Something about: "It takes seven years to cover primary school. Another six for secondary. Three or four for a first degree, and another three for a doctorate."'

'I remember that,' he said.

'You went on to say that if salvation depended upon examination, most people would fail at the entrance to kindergarten, but that we must do better than that.'

He nodded.

'So, I have been listening, and even doing some reading.' She gestured at her bedside table, where Williams recognized a Bible.

'I have also been thinking over my life, with many regrets for things done and undone—undone mainly.'

'Most of us fail there,' he said.

'But we cannot go back,' she said.

'We can't,' he said. 'But I believe that God can take things in our past and make them platforms for the future.'

She sighed gently.

'I thought that that had happened with Harold,' she said. 'I thought that in him, we could make up somehow for what my father had done to Donald, though he did it with my full approval.'

'Are you sure that you want me to know this?' he said, cautioning.

She was silent a moment, then continued.

'You are very wise. It is something which is not necessarily to be brought into knowledge, other than those whom it concerns.' She paused again, then pulled herself up in the bed. 'I think I must change my will,' she said.

'Have you seen Mr Wade?' he asked.

'Yes,' she said quietly. 'He came to see me the next day, and explained what had happened. It was an unfortunate accident. I can think of other similar things when I was a girl. At least two of my father's guests were shot in similar circumstances out on the moor. It is so easy.'

She glanced at him.

'You look puzzled,' she said, almost with a chuckle. 'Did you know that I was a good shot in my time? My father taught me, though it wasn't quite the thing.'

Her fingers plucked the covers again.

'Yes,' she said. 'Yes. If there is a covey coming down-wind between the butts you can forget your neighbours as the birds come between you, and the butts are not all that far apart. I can quite see how it happened.'

There was a light knock at the door and the nurse came in.

'It's all right, Helen,' said the old woman. 'I'm quite all right.'

But the nurse was not convinced, and fussed about the bed. Out of sight of Miss Anthony, she jerked her head in the direction of the door.

Williams took the hint and made his excuses.

Outside, he said to the nurse, 'She seems to be taking it remarkably well.'

'Thanks to Dr Adams,' she said shortly.

'How heavily is she sedated?' asked Williams. 'She didn't seem so to me. She was as sharp as ever.'

The nurse grinned briefly. 'Sharp's the word,' she said. 'She has a tongue that would cut stone if she is displeased by something. But I know what you mean. She is still following things, but she is spending a lot of time living in her memories.'

'Brooding?'

'No. Not really. But there is a stage when they are happier with the things they remember than with things that are happening. The coming of the young man was quite a shock, and it's my opinion she's happier now that he has gone and things are back to what they were.'

'Are they?'

She looked at him, curious.

'Why do you say that?'

'I don't know,' he replied. 'Just something that she said.'

The nurse shrugged it off.

Just then the doorbell rang briefly. The nurse looked at her watch. 'That will be Stella. The night shift,' she explained. 'Do you think you could let her in while I go and get my coat? I want to be away prompt tonight.'

'Yes. Surely,' said Williams.

It was Stella. Williams let her in and set off home himself. There was a car tucked in at the entrance to Hill House. There was someone sitting in it. Williams smiled to himself. That would be why Helen was so anxious to get away on time.

6

'Well, Minister. So you came. Hope you are fit.'

Hughes turned and went back into his small house, beckoning his guest to follow.

Williams did.

'Wait you there,' said Hughes pointing towards a chair in the main room. 'I'll be a minute.' He disappeared upstairs.

Williams heard him clumping about. He thought he heard some conversation, but decided to ignore it. Instead he looked around him.

The place was a mess, as though someone had taken a nice comfortable cottage, added books, magazines, clothes, footwear and the sort of bits and pieces that a boy accumulates over a few years, and stirred. A dry, spindly geranium was struggling for its life on the windowsill. There were bookcases on three walls, wherever there was room. A roll-top desk was in the middle of one wall, letters and papers covering its open top. Beside the fireplace there stood a music-centre that had not been there on Williams's previous visit. It looked expensive. Cassettes and compact discs lay untidy beside it. Twin speakers were on brackets above the bookcases on the other wall. A television was in the corner opposite what was obviously Hughes's chair.

Williams turned to the bookcase behind him. The once or twice he had visited Hughes before, he had never been left on his own, and politeness had prevented the inspection he had longed to carry out.

There was a strange mixture. On the upper shelves he recognized some traditional ancient books, including some of Scott, and some red covers of the Famous British Trials series. There was a single volume of Cockburn's *Journal*. Le Roy Ladurie's *Montaillou* supported a few issues of the *National Geographic*. There were two biographies of Keir Hardie, and one of Harold Wilson's accounts of his time in power. A book on Noritake ware. But the most were paperbacks—Chapman Pincher's *Inside Story* stood next to Boyle's *The Climate of Treason* and a hardback of Rebecca West's *The Meaning of Treason*. Then there were a few of John Norman's 'Gor' series, a couple of Jung's and a do-it-yourself book on psychiatry, Van Loon's *History of Mankind*. On the bottom shelf there were neat piles of Agatha Christies, Dorothy Sayers and P. D. James. There was also a separate pile of Šolzenitsyn, partly in hardback, and a few books on black magic, ghosts and the occult.

'Do you read a lot?' The question surprised Williams. He had not heard Hughes come downstairs.

'Yes, I do,' he replied.

'Not just for your job?'

'No. Though there is a good deal of that.'

Hughes grunted. He went over to the bookcase on the other wall, took out an odd dun cloth-covered book, and gave it to Williams.

Williams recognized it as the 1946 official *History of the Communist Party of the Soviet Union*, the one with the chapter by Stalin.

'Read that?' asked Hughes.

'Yes. I have, actually,' said Williams.

Hughes took it back, and stuffed it again into the bookcase, more or less from where he had taken it out. He pulled out another book and handed it to Williams.

'That?'

It was a biography of Bismarck.

'No.'

'You can take it, if you like.'

'Thank you. He was an interesting man. But perhaps I could pick it up later?'

'Take it now, if you want it.'

Williams looked at the book. It might fit into his haversack. He hefted it, and then put it into his bag.

Hughes watched, expressionless, then turned and went into the kitchen.

He came back almost immediately with his own bag, a camouflage green anorak and a stick.

'Right,' he said.

Williams lifted his bag.

'See your feet?' said Hughes.

Williams pulled up his trouser legs. He had on hiking boots.

'Right,' said Hughes again, and went out through the door. Williams followed him, shutting the door behind him.

Hughes led the way round to the lean-to which protected the Land-Rover from some of the elements.

Hughes drove in silence, throwing the vehicle into the bends on the rough bulldozed track. Williams made one or two attempts at conversation, but was greeted only with a grunt by way of reply. He soon fell silent too, and gave his full attention to not appearing concerned as the Land-Rover powered its way along. He found his right leg moving convulsively not a few times as if he were stamping on the brakes, and at length simply held himself rigid against the back rest by bracing his feet, so as not to be thrown about.

They went up the estate track on the north side of the long valley, towards the Devil's Gate. Williams was kept busy opening the various gates that marked where fences crossed the track. Then they branched off to the right up the Mary Way until they came to Carnloch. There were fewer gates up here. The track was on the east side of the loch, moving quite high above it. The waters were crystal in the early light.

At the top of the loch, the new track led up again to the right for about two miles, running beside a small stream at the base of the encroaching hills, until it petered out in a grassy plot, beside another fence and gate.

Hughes pulled the Land-Rover to a halt.

'Right,' he said. 'Out.'

Williams got out. To his surprise Hughes then drove the vehicle in a circle and came back to stop beside him. He opened the window and said, 'Stay you here. I'll put the beast back down beside the loch. You'll not want to walk here from the Grey Valley, will you?'

'What do you mean?' asked Williams, bewildered.

Hughes looked at him carefully.

'We will be coming down the Grey Valley at the end of the day. I don't think you will be in a fit state to walk all the way up here then.'

'The Grey Valley?'

'The one that runs from the loch to the Grey Hill. The herd is likely in there just now and we'll come down that way.'

'Oh.' Williams thought. 'But then why didn't you leave the Land-Rover there in the first place?'

'You're not as fit as Peter Wade, I'm thinking,' returned Hughes, and drove off.

There was a slight breeze from the south. The valley was cold, the sunshine not yet having warmed it. Williams shivered. The heater in the Land-Rover had been efficient. He looked around. He hadn't been this far up this valley on the valley floor before. There was a clump of birch down beside the stream, and he went over to see if it afforded any shelter from the breeze.

It didn't, but he hunkered down beside the trees and waited. Close by upstream there was a small waterfall, glinting in the sun. A wagtail was hopping about on its stones. He watched it for a while.

Eventually he remembered Bismarck, and pulled it from his haversack. It did not really help.

Hughes was gone about half an hour. He came swinging up the track, brandishing his stick as if he were Drum-Major for a thousand pipers. Williams rose, and went back to the gate.

'Right,' said Hughes. 'Let's go, Minister.'

Williams opened the gate.

'Where are we going?' he asked.

'Yesterday the herd was over to the south of the Grey Valley. I reckon with this wind and the mildness—' Williams shivered but Hughes ignored it—'they will have come into the Grey Valley itself. There's good feeding for

them there just now. We'll go up over there—' he pointed
with his stick—'and sweep round from the north.'

Williams looked at the indicated path. It seemed a
steep, trackless, heathery and grassy wasteland. He mock-
courteously waved his hand, indicating that Hughes should
lead the way.

He shut the gate behind them, and set off in Hughes's
wake. Already he was regretting that airy gesture. Hughes
set a cracking pace.

By the time they stopped for lunch, Williams's regret that
he had let Hughes lead was rock-hard—as were the muscles
in his left calf. He sat, deep in the bowl of heather where
they had stopped, and massaged his leg. His socks were
draped over a heather bush.

'I told you to watch where you put your feet in that bog,'
said Hughes unsympathetically.

'I did,' said Williams.

Hughes grunted.

'I just didn't think that that patch was bog at all. It looked
like firm ground.'

Hughes grunted again, and took a bite from a large
sandwich. Then, as he chomped away at it, he said, 'You've
got to go from tussock to tussock in those places. The clear
bits are where the mud is so deep that nothing will grow.'

'Well, I know that now,' returned Williams stiffly. He
pulled his haversack to him and unpacked his own sand-
wiches. He looked at his muddy hands, and then gloomily
took the drier of his socks and scrubbed the ends of his
fingers—not clean, but cleaner, and then set to work. He
was famished.

'Don't drink too much,' warned Hughes.

It was Williams's turn to nod.

When Hughes was finished, he lay back among the
heather, and in due course Williams copied him.

Below the level of the heather, out of the wind, it was

pleasant. The wind made little rushing noises, and he was conscious of its passing just a few inches above him. The sky was a clear, crystal blue.

A lark began to sing, and, lying there, Williams soon spotted it, a dot against the blue. It went up and up and up.

'Vaughan Williams got that right,' said Hughes suddenly.

'I beg your pardon?' said Williams sitting up.

'Vaughan Williams,' said Hughes impatiently, and also sitting up. He pulled at a grass beside him and stuck it in his mouth. 'Vaughan Williams, "The Lark Ascending". It just goes and goes until . . .' He shrugged, and lay back among the heather.

'You are very interested in music, aren't you?' asked Williams.

'Some,' said Hughes.

'And you read a lot of books.'

Hughes sat up again and grinned, a sly sort of grin.

'Aren't gamekeepers allowed to read?' he asked.

'Of course. Of course.'

'Well, then.' Hughes sprawled himself back down again.

Williams lay down as well, and looked for the lark.

It had gone.

After a few minutes Hughes sat up once more.

'Well,' he said, picking another grass, 'aren't you going to ask me about the accident?'

'I don't think so,' said Williams.

Hughes took the grass stem out of his mouth and played with it, twisting it back and forward in his fingers.

'It was an accident,' he said abruptly.

'So I gather,' said Williams lightly.

'It happens.'

'Yes.'

'Even to the best shots.'

There was a silence between them, which Hughes eventually broke with a chuckle.

'I remember the day I loaded for the best shot I ever saw,' he said, his eyes lighting at the memory. 'He had paid a lot for his week here. They all pay a lot, but damn little of it comes through to the workers.' He sniffed.

Williams waited. This was an old refrain, but Hughes surprised him by not taking it up.

'It was down on the Gannockburn beat,' he went on, gesturing to the south. 'One of the gentlemen had married the most awful pest of a wife. She was a right nuisance to everyone. She was bored stiff with being away up here away from her friends in London. But she was a lively piece.'

He glanced at Williams, who was still staring upwards.

'I think she had been his secretary, but I'm not sure,' he went on. 'Still, this day it was blowing, and for some reason she decided that she was going to come out with the shoot.' He laughed. 'She came out in welly boots and a camel coat, and complained and complained the whole way. She hadn't thought they actually had to walk to the butts, but she couldn't walk home herself.' He stole a glance at Williams, who succumbed. It did sound as if Hughes was about to relate something interesting.

Williams sat up. 'Go on,' he said.

'Well,' said Hughes, 'those birds were coming down-wind round the flank of the Gannock. The wind was doing about thirty miles an hour, and the birds fly at about sixty, so they were going some.'

He paused.

'And?' prompted Williams.

'Well, I knew the Major was a good shot. He had done well on other days, although that morning he hadn't got on too well—it had been having her along, I suppose.'

Hughes got to his feet and gestured round the small depression in the heather that they were sitting in.

'The grouse were coming that way.' He pointed south. 'She was sitting at that left corner supposedly out of the wind. The Major was at the right. And I was behind with the guns.' Hughes was getting enthusiastic.

'When the birds started to show, the Major told her to keep a lookout. So she turned and looked at them coming.' He stopped and looked at Williams.

'I knew something was coming when he winked at me,' said Hughes. He turned and mimicked the action of aiming and firing. Then he turned to Williams.

'He picked off a bird right in front of the butt.'

'Good shooting,' said Williams uncomprehendingly.

Hughes grinned broadly, and closed the trap on the ignorant.

'Good?' he said. 'It was brilliant. That bird died at ninety miles an hour. It fell straight into her face and laid her out stone cold.' He laughed loud. 'We had to get a pony to take her down to the Land-Rover. She was like a gralloched stag draped over it.'

He smacked his lips. 'I saw her two days later before she went off on the train, with dark glasses hiding two lovely black eyes. Serve her right. She didn't belong on the hills. Nice enough in her place—behind a bar, say, but not here in the hills.'

He straightened himself and again went through the motions of aiming.

'Bang,' he said.

Williams got to his feet slowly. He had muscles he had never known of before.

'I thought you told me once you went hill-walking,' said Hughes.

'When I was younger,' said Williams ruefully.

'Mr Wade, now. He goes walking. He's fit,' said Hughes.

'And he can shoot,' said Williams.

Hughes looked carefully at him. 'It was an accident,' he said.

'Yes, I know,' said Williams, bending over to try his socks. They seemed dry enough, and he sat down to put them on.

'Do you get many women coming shooting?' he asked as he struggled with the damp wool.

'Not many,' said Hughes. 'And the few that do are no good. There was one out in the same shoot as with Wade. She spent her time shooting the hares.'

'Are there many of them, hares, I mean?'

'Oh yes. And they do have to get cleared so I suppose she was some use.'

'But you don't approve.'

'No. That's man's work.'

'You'll get the feminists after you for saying that.'

'Feminists,' snorted Hughes in contempt.

Williams shrugged, and started to lace up his boots. His feet felt like blocks of ice in the damp socks. The sooner they got on the move the better.

'Mind you, I do get a lot of women after me,' said Hughes slyly.

Williams said nothing.

'I could have told D. H. Lawrence a lot,' offered Hughes.

'Shall we go?' said Williams.

He was tired but exultant when he got back home. Hughes, the stalker, had proved to be as good as his reputation. When they had got to the down-wind edge of the Grey Valley, and Indian-crawled for a couple of hundred yards to a suitable point, there had been deer only about fifty to sixty yards away, passing along the face of the hill. Williams's one regret was that he had never been able to afford a decent camera with a telephoto lens. His resolve now was to get one as soon as possible. Ann was not pleased to hear that news.

TWO: OCTOBER

As he drove through the twilight to the church Williams thought over the meetings to come. Everywhere, it seemed, the Kirk Session, the gathering of the 'elders' of the congregation, was so much less important than in former centuries, though nominally it was the senior body. It was a comment on the times, and on the church in general, that the council which dealt with spiritual matters had so little authority or effective power. The Board, controlling finance and property, was where the real discussions took place. Perhaps in future years he would manage to change that. In the meantime there was the problem of the proposed Jumble Sale, though he had hopes that that suggestion would fall by the wayside.

The cold blue-silver eyes of a cat showed as he turned off the main road and on to the winding road up to the church. It stared at the intruder and then skulked quickly off into the undergrowth. Clearly it did not have to subsist on kangaroo meat or fish offal. Somewhere its unknowing dinner was already waiting for it.

He drove on. Once more he found himself regretting that the forefathers of the village had placed the church so far away. Still, the church had been in the valley before the village. Though the present buildings were only a hundred or so years old, there had been a church on that site for at least three centuries. But if only the fire of 1846 had been taken as an excuse for re-siting the church . . . It would have been so much better to have had the church actually in the village. Or if the chance had been taken to build in the square when the village was being laid out, the church could have been a focus for the layout of the community. That would have made it easier for it to be a part of the life of the community. Instead, perched on its small hill a mile down the valley, and a quarter of a mile from the main road, the church was isolated. While it certainly had an outlook, and could be seen from all over the parish, which had doubtless been the justification of the site in the past, nowadays the distance seemed a barrier between the church and the people. It was apart, just as the church general was apart from the real life of the people. Indeed, as someone had said to him as he had made his first visits when he was settling in, its apartness seemed like a condemnation, as if perched on its little hill the church looked down on the village.

He gave himself to the swings and curves of the drive. There was something hypnotic about the movement, swishing past the old elms on either side. Then, at a gap in the trees he saw the church: the buildings were dark against the darkness of the evening. The rota for opening up looked as though it had not worked.

Sure enough, as he entered the car park, there were several parked cars, their occupants waiting.

He drew to a halt and got out. As he pulled up, the others got out of their cars and came towards the building. Then Peter Wade's distinctive white car came up the drive and parked in its usual place. Wade got out. Williams noticed that he did not bother to lock his car.

'You haven't locked it,' he called.

'Safe enough here,' returned the other.

They went in to the meeting.

'Might I suggest,' said Wade smoothly, 'that we simply call for motions and counter-motions?'

Williams looked round the small room at the so-called leaders in his congregation. He felt trapped. This was not the way that he had intended things to go. He had had high hopes coming to the Session Room. But the roots of the Jumble Sale—the 'Spring Fayre' they seemed to want to call it—were too deep. Too deep? Surely not *too* deep. But he had mistaken the achievements of his ministry. Certainly there were many in the congregation who would have clearly understood his feelings and would have followed his leadership even if they did not fully comprehend his reasons for acting, nor share them if they did. But here, among these hardened men, he had now to act for the future. The present battle was lost, lost precisely because he had not appreciated that it was a battle. But now he knew there was a war on, and next time . . .

'No,' he said. 'No. I do not think that that will be necessary.'

He let the silence stretch a little. It would do them good to realize that he was not to be pushed around.

'No,' he resumed, picking up his pencil and carefully balancing it on its end. 'We won't have formal motions and votes on this. The feeling of the meeting is clear. We will have a Spring Fayre next March. I would much rather have our meetings run by consensus rather than on voting. But perhaps we will reconsider matters further at this time next year.'

'Shall I minute that?' asked Wade.

'I don't think so,' replied Williams.

'If I might say something, Minister?' The voice belonged to a large, weatherbeaten figure.

'Surely,' said Williams.

'I am not happy,' said the figure. 'It seems to me that we should trust what our minister feels. I would propose that we do not have a Jumble Sale next year. I think he's right. If you are to give money to God, or to the Church, you should just give it and not ask for something back.' He paused, and struggled with an idea: then it came out in a rush. 'You can't sell your money to God. It's not right.'

'Thank you, Andrew,' said Williams gently, but immediately. 'I appreciate your feelings, but for the present we should do what we have usually done. Another time, perhaps?' He tapped the balanced pencil, and it fell over with a clatter.

'Now,' he said. 'Is there any other business?'

Most of the cars had gone when Williams came out from the church buildings, but Wade's Mercedes was still there, its white prominent in the darkened car park. Wade got out of it and came up to Williams. 'If I might have a word,' he said.

Williams smiled his assent.

'I hate to ask this, Minister,' Wade said, 'but I wonder if it is entirely wise to conduct meetings as informally as we seem to be getting into the habit of. It is not businesslike. And I must say that some of the older men are somewhat uncomfortable at being called by their Christian names during official meetings of the Session.'

'Peter,' said Williams, 'we have to be a family. That is what the church is supposed to be. And families don't call each other Mr this and Mr that. It's unnatural. Now I do know that behaving like that at a Session or Board meeting is still unfamiliar to most of us, but that is not the same as saying it's wrong. And I must say I do believe that if we can learn to talk to each other without formality and behave as family, it will help things get done pleasantly.'

He looked at Wade as he spoke, but Wade had turned his head to look down the valley, and Williams could not make out his expression.

'I will bear what you say in mind,' he added placatingly. 'But I would ask you to think over what I have said too.' He moved over towards his car when the other made no reply.

'Indeed, I will, Minister,' said Wade suddenly. He paused and then said, 'It's a fine night.'

Williams accepted the olive branch. He walked back

across to where Wade stood. The moon was well on the wane, but the valley was still lit by it. The sky was clear, with stars twinkling here and there.

'I used to enjoy star-gazing,' he said, looking up. 'It's good to live out here, away from the city lights. You forget the glories of creation in the lights of the towns.'

'Nice and quiet,' said Wade.

'I remember once I thought I had seen a Flying Saucer,' said Williams reflectively. 'Two, in fact.'

Wade turned his head.

'I was at the top end of my mother's garden, using a pair of Victorian opera glasses. I saw these two objects, shaped just like rugby balls seen side on, and they were where I knew there should not be any stars. I had done enough star-gazing to know that. I galloped into the house to find my star book and dashed out again, and there they still were, in the same place, but they seemed to be going up and down.'

Wade seemed to be politely interested.

'But then I looked without the glasses. What I was seeing were the insulators on the man next door's wireless aerial. He worked in the trawling business and had a powerful radio to listen in to trawler messages. I was seeing the insulators on his aerial, not an Invasion of Earth at all.' Williams chuckled.

Wade said nothing. The two turned their attention back to the skies, Williams somewhat embarrassed by the unexpected enthusiasm which had risen in him, and by having let Wade see it.

A meteor flashed.

'Goodness,' said Williams. 'I haven't seen one of those for years.'

'Bad luck,' said Wade.

'Have you seen many?' asked Williams.

'No. But that's not what I meant. They say that a falling star is bad luck. It means a death.'

'Oh, come now, Peter,' said Williams. 'You cannot believe in all that superstitious rubbish.'

Wade did not reply.

Another meteor flashed, this time a green streak against the glittering stars. Williams grunted in surprise. 'I wonder what it is?' he said. 'There are meteor showers at various times. I seem to remember that there are the . . . the . . . No, it won't come. But there are clusters of meteors that follow certain paths round the sun, like comets, and come every year at about the same dates.'

Wade stood, looking up, saying nothing.

'Unless it was a bit of a satellite, or space debris,' mused Williams. 'They say that there are lots of bits burn up every year.'

Wade snorted. 'I read somewhere recently that some of them make it back to earth. Could be a neat legal claim in that.'

'What an awful thought,' said Williams.

'But it would be quick,' replied Wade. 'Something like that must be going a fair speed.' He shivered, then pulled himself together. He made a show of looking at his watch. Williams saw the glint of gold as he pulled back his sleeve.

'Well,' he said briskly. 'That time already. I had better be on my way. See you on Sunday, Minister.' He got into his car, switched on the lights, started the car and drove off.

Williams looked after him. 'Must tell him his rear offside light has gone,' he mused. He watched the flare of Wade's lights go down the twisting drive. 'One of these days he's going to misjudge things . . .' Wade's driving was notorious, his reputation bolstered by at least one conviction for speeding. Williams shrugged, and surveyed the quiet, moon-dark valley once more. The lights of Wade's car appeared out on the main road, tunnelling their way towards the river and Bridge House, where Wade lived his bachelor life.

'Confound the man. No, I don't mean that. What do I mean? Too tired. Time for home,' he muttered.

Another meteor flashed.

'I wonder where my astronomy book has gone. Sidgwick, wasn't it? Sidgwick, *Introducing Astronomy*.' He smiled as his mind brought back the memory of childhood.

He got into his car and set off down the drive. Remembering Wade's progress, he grinned at his own sedate speed as he took the curves.

THREE: MARCH

1

The day of the Spring Fayre was fine, though spring itself had been late in coming that year. A few clouds dotted the blue sky, and the air did hold the promise of the spring to come as Williams wandered down to one of the open-air events. Things seemed to be going well.

'Pull!' The voice was gruff.

'Spang . . . Spangg!' The two target discs sped across the face of the clearing in front of the trees. The beefy figure tracked the muzzle of the shotgun. There was one 'bang' quickly followed by another, and then the gun was broken and the cartridges ejected over the man's shoulder. He fumbled in his pocket and reloaded.

'He's like a gun-turret in a battleship,' whispered Williams to Peter Wade.

'He is a good shot,' returned the other primly.

The procedure was repeated. And again. But on the third repeat the left-hand target was unscathed.

'Ah well, Peter,' said the man turning with a smile on his face. 'You still have the best of it.'

'No,' said Wade. 'In the competition Henry Maddon has done best so far.'

'Have you disqualified yourself, then?' asked the other. 'I suppose if you're not competing then others will have a chance. Why didn't you tell me?'

Wade shrugged.

The big man grinned. Then he said to Williams, 'Come

on, Minister. You must have a shot as well.

'Oh no, Colin,' said Williams. 'I've never shot a gun.'

'Come on,' said the other, holding out the gun. 'After all, this is all in aid of the church. I'll pay.'

'No,' said Williams. 'I couldn't let you do that . . .' but his objections were swept aside.

Colin Marsh said, 'I've still got two shots left in my five quid. You can have one of them, and if you actually hit the target, I'll give another twenty pounds as a donation.'

Williams could think of no polite way out of it, and so, shortly afterwards he stood, gun to shoulder, waiting. He had bargained the trial down to a single disc, and the others had suggested that tracking to the left might be easier than tracking to the right. Accordingly he was expecting the disc to rise from the right-hand trap.

'Pull,' he shouted.

'Spangg!'

'Bang.'

Williams dropped the gun and grabbed his right shoulder.

'Minister, Minister,' said the big man, coming over anxiously. 'I warned you to keep the butt hard against your shoulder.'

'I forgot,' said Williams through clenched teeth.

'It gives some kick,' said the other. 'You'll have a nice bruise tomorrow.'

Wade had picked up the gun and stood, cleaning its stock with a handkerchief.

'I am sorry, Peter,' said Williams. 'I hope I haven't damaged your gun.'

Wade said nothing until he had carefully examined the piece. Then he said, 'No, it's all right. It's just as well you dropped it butt-first.'

Williams looked anxiously at him. Wade smiled.

'No. It landed on the grass .which meant it was not scratched. If it had gone down muzzle-first, it might have picked up dirt.'

He turned easily, reloading the gun.

'Pull,' he called.

'Bang!' The disc disintegrated very shortly after its appearance above the bank of earth which protected the operator of the trap.

'What's the record?' came a voice.

Wade turned. Evan Hughes was coming into the clearing.

'Can I have a turn?' he said, striding forward.

'It's a pound for four shots,' said Wade.

'A pound?' said Hughes, incredulously.

'A pound.'

Hughes snorted.

'It's in a good cause,' said the large man.

Hughes spat. 'Religious rubbish. I just came down to see if there was anything interesting in the sale. But I never thought you would be charging like that. That's diabolical.'

He turned on his heel and went off.

Williams looked after him, massaging his shoulder.

'Come on, Minister,' said the large man. 'We'll need to have a look at that shoulder. Can you raise your arm?'

After Williams had moved his shoulder about a bit, and after some inexpert prodding by Colin Marsh, the conclusion was that nothing was broken.

'At least, I don't think so,' said Marsh. He was, however, clearly worried.

'It's not your fault,' said Williams. 'Your instructions were very clear.'

Wade smiled. Marsh saw it, and his face darkened.

'No. It was my fault,' said Williams. 'I just got too excited.'

'Well, come on back to the church hall and I'll buy you a cup of coffee, at least,' said Marsh.

'I'll wait here for more clients,' said Wade. He turned and went over to the trap operator, who had been watching from behind his mound.

Williams and Marsh left the plantation and crossed the

road, went along it for a couple of hundred yards and then
turned into the church drive. About half way up they met
a pony led by a youngish woman and carrying a child on
its back.

'Come on, Harry,' said Williams to the boy. 'How about
you getting off and letting me have a turn?'

The child giggled.

'Come, come, Minister,' said the woman. 'If you want
to ride you'll need to come to the stables and get fitted
out with a proper horse, not a wee pony like this.' She
laughed.

'Betty Robertson,' said Marsh. 'Are you never tired of
drumming up business for that stable of yours?'

''Course not,' said the woman. 'That's how to build it
up.'

'Someday, perhaps,' said Williams.

Back at the church Marsh and Williams settled into a corner
table in the small hall. The hall was satisfactorily full, and
they sat, backs against the wall, looking out at the convivial
scene.

'You'll forgive me, Minister,' said Marsh slowly as they
waited for their coffee to be brought from the kitchen. 'I still
cannot see what your objection to the Spring Fayre was.'
He motioned to the rest of the hall. 'It brings people happily
together. It gets them working together in a good cause. It
makes money for the church.'

Williams said nothing immediately, but did not allow the
silence to become painful.

'It's like this,' he said gently. 'You remember what old
Andrew said at the Session meeting?'

'Yes?'

'That was it, in just a few simple sentences. I believe that
we should not do something like this for the benefit of the
church. In fact were things going well, I do not think we
would have need of such things at all. People would give

money without being asked if Christ were really touching them.'

Marsh shook his head. He was just about to say something when there was a commotion in the large hall. They heard shouting, and something falling.

When they had got through the small hall and into the larger one, they found a man picking himself up out of a muddle on the floor. He had fallen into the Cake and Candy stall. It had collapsed. Behind the stall a middle-aged matron was having hysterics. Other people were standing round. The outside door of the hall slammed.

Ann came towards Williams.

'I'll explain later,' she said, and went to the distraught woman.

'What's wrong, Mr Maddon?' Williams said to the man, who had now got to his feet and was brushing crumbs and debris from his suit.

'That swine,' said Maddon, purpling. 'He hit me,' he went on in an almost puzzled voice.

'What?' said Williams.

'It's true,' said one of the bystanders. 'It was that Hughes. He hit Mr Maddon.' She fumbled in her handbag for a handkerchief.

'You had better come through to the vestry,' Williams said to Maddon. 'Can you help straighten this out?' he added to Colin Marsh.

'Fairly that, Minister,' replied Marsh, bending to locate the legs of the collapsed table.

'I am quite all right,' said Maddon indignantly. 'But I am going to get in touch with the police. Something must be done about that man. You were all witnesses.' He looked round the immediate group.

One of these was Mrs Jenkins. She said in a businesslike voice, 'I quite agree that something has to be done. But it was you, Mr Maddon, who hit Mr Hughes first.'

Maddon spluttered. 'I had every reason to,' he began.

'And so you have,' cut in Mrs Jenkins. 'But it means that you assaulted him, and not the other way round.'

Maddon glared at her.

'I am sure that Mr Maddon has much truth on his side,' said Williams, taking Maddon by the elbow, 'but perhaps we could review this situation quietly?'

'Rubbish,' said Maddon angrily, twisting out of his grasp. 'Come, Mavis.' He swept out of the hall, a dowdy matron in his wake.

2

'What was that all about?' Williams said later to Ann, safe in the peace of their own house.

'It was all quite melodramatic,' said Ann. 'That man Hughes came into the hall and was poking about the Bric-à-Brac, when Henry Maddon saw him. He went straight over to him and hit him. He was saying something, but I did not catch it. And Hughes simply gave him a huge push and he ended up on the Cake and Candy.'

'In the Cake and Candy, more like,' Williams grinned.

Ann chuckled, but then quickly sobered.

'It's no laughing matter. I gather from what you said among the ladies afterwards that the problem is that Hughes has got Maddon's daughter Iris in the family way.'

'Oh no!'

'I'm afraid so. It has been a great shock to the Maddons, and they are such respectable folk. It must be a very great hurt.'

Williams nodded. 'I had better go and see them.'

'Not yet. They'll be horribly embarrassed at having made a scene. Give them time to settle. Or even wait until they come to see you.'

'Or you.'

'Yes. I suppose that's more likely.'

'I am surprised that Maddon would get so worked up, even about something like that.'

'Well, you can see it, if you think about it. Iris is their only child and has been the apple of their eye.'

'Has she finished school?'

'Yes. Or at least she will be, and was to be going to the University in autumn.'

'And now?'

'I have no idea. Needless to say the ladies were not too forthcoming to the minister's wife, though I could see that one or two seemed to know all about it.'

'Or were pretending to?'

'Perhaps.'

'There's nothing like a small community for gossip.'

'I know. I wonder sometimes what they think of your having gone to see Hughes so often.'

'What! Four or five visits?'

'I know that. But you never know what they are thinking. One of the ladies was quite sniffy this afternoon after you had gone back into the small hall.'

'Who?'

'I'm not sure. It was behind my back, but quite audible. Something like, "The minister *would* stand up for *him*." And there was no doubt from the tone who the "him" was.'

'Oh dear,' said Williams gloomily. 'People.'

'Your flock, my dear.'

'Too many black sheep,' said Williams.

'And one goat,' smiled Ann.

3

Williams was singing to himself as he drove along the tunnel of light. This time it was Brahms. As usual, the singing meant he was in a good mood, though, as he asked himself, why that should be was obscure. The Session meeting was likely to be 'difficult', for it was certain that the question of Hughes and Maddon would come up.

There was no cat at the entry to the church road. Briefly he wondered where it was, and what unwary prey it would catch that night. Hunting and hunters: was it really necessary? He shook his head as he drove up the winding road, lined by its creaking elms. He weaved his way between the trees—just like an uphill slalom, he thought. Appropriate too: the meeting to come would be an uphill job.

He caught a glimpse of the church at the open bend. The lights were on in the Hall, so the rota for its opening for Session meetings must have worked, he thought with relief. Usually his Session or Board were diplomatic, but it didn't help to have things break down in that way. But as he approached and saw Wade's car parked in its usual place at the lower edge of the car park facing the road as if ready to make a swift exit, he remembered. He had had no need to worry: it was Wade's turn on the opening rota.

As Williams pulled his car round and into its accustomed place beside the door to the vestry he remembered something else. Another statistical return had to be made to church offices, and he did not have the information himself. Perhaps he would be able to discuss it with Peter Wade before the meeting began. Wade would be sure to know. And yet . . . Williams found himself wondering once more why Wade bothered. He seemed detached and uninterested in any real church matters. His forte was formal business, getting the statistics right, and making the minutes as bland as could be, yet he always lingered after meetings, talking to various members of the Session, and sometimes to Williams himself. Perhaps it was a matter of 'business'— among the farming community there sometimes was expensive business to be done. On the other hand, Williams felt sure that Wade's main business came from Greyhavens itself. He seemed to live well—better than business originating only in the parish of PenIron would have explained, even given Miss Anthony, Mrs Jenkins and one or two others.

He was right about the meeting. The report from Keith Robertson, the Convener of the Fayre, was good news—in financial terms. Some fifteen hundred pounds would be making its way into the church funds in due course after the expenses had been settled. But, as Williams told himself, that only meant that it would be the more difficult to convince these men that that method of church financing was undesirable. He could tell as much from the self-satisfied smirk with which the news was conveyed to the meeting.

It was old Isaac Watson who raised the question of Hughes.

'Even so,' he said, interrupting Robertson, 'the Fayre was not trouble-free, and I'm sure that that had something to do with it not being right.' He rolled the 'r' of 'right'.

'That was unfortunate,' replied Robertson. 'However, I do not see that it had anything to do with the Fayre. I really don't want to comment on that,' he continued after looking around him, 'especially in the absence of our good friend Henry Maddon.'

There was a murmur of approval at this, and Williams felt he had to say something.

'I think, gentlemen, that Keith is right. We should not talk of what happened in the absence of Mr Maddon.'

'It's that Hughes that is the trouble,' said another voice. 'He's a wrong 'un. Cannot we do something about him to stop him coming round and spoiling our church affairs? My wife is sure he took things from her stall last Fayre, and you remember he was drunk at the Watch-night service one year.'

Williams moved to block this off.

'It would be better if we did not discuss such matters,' he said, getting to his feet and looking round them all. 'I recall no complaints about Mr Hughes in the time that I have been here. And we must remember that the church is for everyone who will come to it. Even if Mr Hughes comes to only the Fayre just now, perhaps that will change as he finds people accept him.'

There was a murmur at this, and Williams realized that he was in a minority on the matter.

'Been visiting him again, have you?' said a speaker Williams could not precisely identify.

'I will—I must—visit every house in the parish. That is my responsibility. And if I am asked to return I will,' he said. 'But I think this item of business has been aired as much as it needs to be. I would thank most warmly, first yourself, Keith—' he turned to the Convener—'and also you, Ian—' he turned to the Church Treasurer—'and all the others who worked so hard for the success of the Fayre.' He paused while there was a mild stamping of feet in approval of what he had said.

'Now. I believe that the Buildings Convener has something to say about the state of the guttering.'

After it was all over, Williams felt very tired. There had been no real animosity, but it had been a drain upon him, he realized, as he pushed his folders into his worn old briefcase, put off the lights, locked the doors and made his way out to the car park. There were only a few cars left.

Wade was talking to Robertson as he came out. Robertson carefully turned his back on the vestry door, and said a few words to Wade before crossing quickly to his car.

Wade strolled back up to him.

'I thought you handled that well,' he said abruptly.

'Thank you. We mustn't get too worked up, or let an isolated occurrence upset things.'

Wade nodded. 'He's an odd man.'

'Hughes?'

'Yes.'

'Yes. But he's an interesting man too.'

'I assume that you know why Maddon was upset?'

'I know a reason.'

'It's true. Hughes has written to me offering to pay aliment for the child provided that there is a court decree against him.'

'Court?'

'Yes. If there is a decree, then it is a proper and lawful debt for the purposes of the Tax authorities. It would reduce his income tax liability. If he just pays up without being forced to in that way he would pay out of taxed income.'

'I don't understand anything of those matters,' said Williams thankfully.

'Well, I just wanted to be sure you knew, in case it helped.'

'Thanks.'

Wade waved his hand and strode off down to his car.

Williams opened the door of his car, threw in his briefcase and got in. Then he remembered that he needed to take home his copy of the Jerusalem Bible, which he had used during the previous Sunday morning service. He got out of the car once more, and went into the church. As he unlocked the door, out of the corner of his eye he saw Wade switch on his powerful beams and set off down the winding road.

Three or four minutes later Williams followed.

He put on his tape once more and began to sing. He was happy again. But only briefly.

He saw the lights from some little way above them. The powerful beams were shining out across the field to the right of the road. Wade must have stopped, he thought. Deer perhaps? But as Williams slalomed round the bend immediately above, he found Wade's white car off the road, its front raised by impact against a tree, the beams shining round the trunk.

Williams stopped, ran to the car and tugged open the driver's door. Wade was sitting, dazed, behind the wheel.

'It wouldn't stop,' he mumbled.

Williams reached across Wade in an attempt to release

the seat-belt, but as he did so the added weight made the car slip slightly.

'I'll do it,' said Wade feebly, pushing Williams away. He released the catch and fell sideways into Williams's grasp. Williams held him a moment and then helped him gently out of the vehicle.

'Better come back a little,' said Williams, guiding the stumbling man. He helped him take a few paces, but then Wade seemed to crumple down—not a fall, but uncannily as if someone had pulled the bung from a blow-up man.

Williams eased him to the ground and went back to his own car for a travelling rug.

He draped it round Wade, and they remained there for some minutes, Wade flat on the tarmac, and Williams first squatting and then standing as the strain got to his calves.

It was eerie. The wind sighed across the grass of the fields, and rustled through the elms. The headlight beams were like searchlights aimed to catch low-flying intruders. A dripping noise began from the car, and got louder as the pool grew.

'Can you move?' asked Williams at length.

Wade sat up shakily, and then moved on to all fours. Then with Williams's help he got to his feet.

Williams guided him over to his own car, and got him into it. He looked back at Wade's car, wondering whether to try to put the lights off, but decided against it. That drip sounded ominous and the car had moved once when he had been close.

He got in at his own side, skirted Wade's car and drove carefully to the manse.

There he left Wade and went in.

Ann was in the kitchen, darning.

'I'm afraid there's been an accident,' he said without preamble. 'Peter Wade has hit a tree. I've got him outside in my car, but he is pretty shaken. Could you phone the

Greyhavens Hospital and I'll take him straight in to Emergency.'

'Oh, Ted. What happened?'

'I don't know. We were the last. He left a minute or so ahead of me, because I had forgotten a book, and when I came down there he was wrapped round one of the elms on the steep bend. The car's a mess. He needs to see a medic soon.'

'All right. Are you sure you're all right?'

'Yes. I'm fine.'

'Wait,' she said, going across to a cupboard. She rummaged in a couple of tins, and gave him some biscuits, and a can of lemonade.

'You'll maybe need this. It'll be ages before you get back.'

He smiled and kissed her forehead. 'I don't know what I would do without you. But you could also phone Douglas Milne at the garage and ask him to cope with the wreck. I didn't want to go near it, and the lights are still on.'

'Do you need anything for Peter?'

'I'll take a couple of travelling rugs from the front room.'

'All right.'

Together they got the rugs and went out to the car.

'Peter! I'm so sorry,' said Ann.

Peter Wade tried to smile, but did not make it. He looked grey.

'You'd better go,' said Ann.

'OK. I'll phone,' Williams replied.

4

Wade was going to be all right. The duty doctor had admitted him to hospital for thirty-six hours just to check that there were no after-effects. So, next morning, it was Williams who had the job of seeing to the arrangements.

Before he drove in to Greyhavens to pass on Wade's messages for his staff, he called in at the garage to ask whether the Milnes had managed to recover the car.

It was there, standing beside a few other wrecks.

Milne saw him looking at them, and came over.

'Pretty messy, aren't they?' he said, wiping oily hands on some cotton waste.

'I'll say,' Williams replied. 'I'm surprised that the people survived.' He kicked a tyre of one battered van.

'Not all of them did.'

'I hadn't realized you had so many.'

'Didn't use to. But since we got taken on as an AA recognized breakdown garage, the police call us out for most of the accidents over on the main road.'

'What about Wade's car?'

Milne grunted and led Williams over to it.

'There's a problem there,' he said.

Williams looked at the car. Its front bore the scars of the tree. The bonnet was sprung.

'He was lucky,' said Milne. 'The engine didn't shift, and presumably he had on his driving belt.'

'Yes, he had on his belt. It was a bit awkward getting him out of it.' Williams hesitated. 'What do you mean about the engine?'

'He hit that tree hard enough to stove in the front and radiator. It's only the engine bolts that stopped the engine from ending up in the driver's seat.'

'Oh.'

'There's something else.'

Milne squatted beside the front offside wheel and pointed.

Williams squatted beside him. He could detect nothing. He knelt: Ann would forgive him—they were his second-best slacks.

'That brake nipple has been crushed, and so has the one on the other side.'

Williams stood up, dusting down his knees. To his dismay,

his right knee was marked and he had made it worse. 'You mean?'

'That car's been got at.'

'Are you sure? Couldn't the impact have done it?'

'Well, perhaps. But it's unlikely.'

'But a car like this! Hasn't it got dual brake circuits and warning lights and all that.'

Milne nodded. He eased the bonnet up with difficulty and pointed again. 'That wire's been pulled off. The warning light wouldn't work with it like that.'

'But how . . .' began Williams, and then corrected himself. 'I suppose that would be easy enough. Peter never locked his car in the church car park.'

'Damn fool,' said Milne.

'Have you told the police?'

'Not yet.'

'Well, I think you had better.'

'What about Wade?'

Briefly, Williams noted the use of the surname. Odd for those who had been boys in the village together. Then he checked: no, Wade must be some eight or nine years older. But even so . . .

'I'll tell him when he is fitter. There may be nothing to it.'

'Maybe.'

'You let the police know, and they can check things out.'

On his way in to Greyhavens Williams went up to the church. There were two areas of brown/green staining on the tarmac, running off into the grass at the side, just where Wade's car had been parked.

He rubbed his finger in one, and smelled it.

On his way back down to the main road, he drove carefully, imagining what it must have been like.

The road had a certain rhythm to it. He chuckled briefly, remembering his thoughts of last night and the way Wade

usually swung down the road. It was indeed like doing a
slalom. Left. Right. Left. Right; and so on. But as it
steepened, he had to brake. He imagined Wade, pumping
at the pedal. Or did it just go smoothly down to the floor,
with no effect? He didn't know.

Ahead of him was the scarred tree.

He got out and looked at it. The bark had shifted from
fully one half of the tree. Yet, he thought, they might be
able to save it. He would come back that afternoon with
twine and a pot of creosote. In the meantime he pulled back
as much bark as he could, and patted it into place.

5

At Wade's office Williams gave the news. The senior assistant, Miss Rettie, a dowdy woman in her late thirties,
seemed not very worried by the accident to her employer,
merely asking whether Mr Wade would be able to sign
cheques.

Williams reassured her, and passed on the other messages
about certain letters to be written and one or two to be
contacted by phone.

'Did he say anything about London?'

'No.'

'Hmmm. I'd better get in touch.'

Williams shrugged. 'I'm sure he will be out and about
soon.'

'Well, perhaps. But there was a phone call this morning
already about some stocks and shares.'

'Does he do a lot of that sort of work?'

'Not on his own, of course. We're lawyers, not stock-
brokers. But there are one or two clients for whom he makes
investment decisions, and there is something in the wind
just now with that privatization, you know.'

Williams didn't, but let the matter pass.

'Shall I tell him? I could go in on my way back home. Ministers have free access to the hospital.'

'I hadn't realized you were a minister. I thought you were a neighbour.'

Williams looked down at himself, and smiled. 'No reason you should have.'

The assistant seemed to relax. 'You know,' she said, 'I once thought of going into the church as my career.'

Williams smiled. He had never thought of the church as a 'career'.

'Yes. I was going through University just when the rules changed and women ministers were allowed. I gave it serious thought. It still concerns me, you know,' said the assistant. She pursed her lips. 'There's too big a gap between what the law allows and proper morals.'

'Yes. We're standing in to danger.'

'In fact I'm quite appalled by some of the things the church lets Parliament get away with. The morals of the country are falling apart. Government just doesn't give a lead, and the church says nothing.'

Williams looked politely interested. Clearly Miss Rettie had a hobby-horse.

'It all started with doing away with capital punishment, and all that sociological rubbish about crime. No one is to be punished. It's all someone else's fault, if fault is the right word at all. Those sociologists have a lot to answer for. They've got no true basis to work from. Most of them are atheists. Look at them giving illegitimate children succession rights to their parents. Then there's all this rubbish about irretrievable breakdown of marriage.'

'You mean divorce is too easy? I would agree with that. But some of the fault there is that the church has never properly explained what is involved in marriage.'

'That's true,' she said. 'But there is also the matter of who is at fault. It's just not true that marriage breaks down.

Someone breaks it down. It's always someone's fault.'

Williams noted that she was ringless, and wondered what might lie behind the heated delivery of these opinions. But she seemed consciously to put a lid on things.

'They've made it pointless to have a marriage. What sort of encouragement is that to taking responsibilities? Now illegitimate children have the same rights as legitimate ones. There's all sorts of grants for the "single-parent family", and everyone leans over backwards for the underprivileged. But if you're married you're worse off. You deal with juveniles by hauling the whole family before a tribunal, and sorting through the whole family affairs by social workers. Social workers!' The word was clearly one of abuse.

'I'm afraid I don't know what you're talking about,' said Williams. Miss Rettie caught his tone, and started to simmer down.

'They've extended their rights. Rights!'

'Oh,' said Williams, none the wiser. 'What do you think the church should have done?'

'Protested. All that sounds good and compassionate, but it down-grades the sanctity of marriage.'

'I suppose so, but there is little authority left to the church now. It pretends it has a significant voice, but if you look at things it really isn't. Perhaps it is coming to realize that.'

'Maybe,' she said, her attention clearly passing on to other things in view of the lack of sympathy she was encountering. 'There's nothing we can do about that here and now, is there?'

Williams shook his head.

'Well,' she said, standing up and holding out her hand, 'thanks for coming in and letting us know. We would have been wondering by now what had happened to Peter.' She glanced at a clock on the wall. 'He's always in by ten.'

FOUR: APRIL

1

It was the dog that found the body and so spoiled a perfect day.

Jack Foster was an absentee father for most of the week. He left early for the office and got home late at night. Once his eldest son had got hold of his diary and in solemn round childish print had entered an appointment in it. 'Take Jim futbol,' it had said. But unfortunately the appointment had been for a Thursday afternoon.

He had shown it to Shona in amusement, and then had retreated in the face of her anger. He had not realized just how little the family had seen of him in these last years since (according to her) he had got drunk on price/earnings ratios. At her invitation, though not within her sight, he had sat down and worked out just how long they had spent together as a family since Stephanie had been born. It had been salutary, as had the realization as he looked at the sleeping faces that evening to realize how his children had grown while he had not noticed.

'You're losing their childhood,' she had railed. 'They'll not want you when you want them, if they can't have you when they want you.'

He had resolved that Sunday at least would be for the family.

They parked the car at the lay-by on the North road and, with Jack carrying the rucksack with the lunch, they made their way up the shooters' path that wound up the shoulder of the Grey Hill. The Grey Hill, the Grey Valley, thought Foster, as he strode on. He had populated so much of their terrain with elves and gnomes, rabbits and dragons, heroes and maidens in distress. Over there, where the green grass revealed the presence of a spring, the Lady of the Green Mantle had encountered the troll, and had been saved by Achilles McGregor From-Bon. On the other side of the track was the spinney where Adolphus the Wee, King of the Rabbits, had directed the attack on Gnomedom, and had come within an inch of losing his fine powder-puff of a tail through being too saucy at the expense of Min the Malevolent.

The day was clear, that clearness after rain when the horizon and distant hills are sharp and seem almost close enough to touch. The sky was cerulean blue; the air, sweet with the fulfilled promise of spring. It was April.

Yes, his bargain had been worth it. There was Jim, running ahead with Lucky, the Golden Retriever, while behind him Shona and Stephanie were talking about something to do with school. They were a family once more.

They had lunch at Stonehenge, the Standing Stones of Maurim. The Stones were not really standing, nor was there any real resemblance to Stonehenge, but it was their name for the place. There was, however, enough of an abruptness about how the Stones rose from the heather to make it a stretchable point. From the small windbreak which the Stones afforded, they looked down the valley before them, down to the tarn that occupied its junction with the larger valley which ran north into the highlands. Foster had promised himself that, one day when Jim was bigger, he would get Shona to drop the two of them back at the lay-by on the main road. They would climb up to Stonehenge, and then down the valley, turn left, go up the Devil's Gate to its end, and then cross over by a path that was indicated, on the maps at least, to the top of the Black Lake. At the other end of that, Shona and Stephanie could collect them in the car park. It would take a long time, but the long days of summer would make it possible, he felt sure.

'Can we go down a way?' asked Jim, as he finished his can of Coke. 'We could go down to the Nether Gate and see whether there are any traces of trolls.'

His mother frowned.

'Oh, come on, Mum,' cried Stephanie. 'I want to see if my troll trap has caught anything.'

'Your troll trap?' said her mother, bewildered.

Foster laughed. 'Imagine you remembering that,' he chuckled, ruffling his daughter's hair with an affectionate hand.

'It must have been when we were here back last September or so, we went down, you remember, and Steffy laid out a trap for trolls with silver paper.'

'That's right,' said the girl. 'Daddy said that a troll would be so surprised to see a face in a piece of silver paper that he would forget the danger of the rising sun, and we would find him turned to stone the next time we came. Oh, please, Mummy. Please.'

Her mother laughed at the intensity of the appeal.

'Not me,' she said. 'I've had enough. But you three can go down if you want. I'll set off back for the car and wait for you there. I brought a book, just in case.'

Foster was immediately concerned. 'It's not been too much for you, has it?' he asked.

'No, no,' she replied. 'It's been three weeks since the flu', but I think I don't want to go down there and then come all the way up again.' She pointed down the steeping sides of the valley which terminated in a curve below them.

'All right,' he said. 'We'll not be long. It still gets dark early.'

She blew a kiss to the children who had started off down the hill as soon as the decision was clear to them. The retriever forayed ahead of the small figures, casting about after rabbit scent.

There was no troll in the trap—not that Foster had expected one. Stephanie was disappointed, and started to remake it carefully according to the instructions given months previously. Six larger stones with pebbles between formed a star shape. Smaller stones were placed on top of each of the larger. In the middle a pile of three stones held the lure, a piece of silver paper held beneath the topmost stone. She had her tongue between her teeth, frowning with concentration.

The dog loped off to the right, in among tussocky heather which had somehow escaped when the area had been burned some years previously. It was too deep for the animal, which had to resort to bounding up and down to make her way.

She started to bark.

'Here, Lucky. Here,' called Foster.

There was no response.

'Oh, go and get that blessed animal,' he said testily to Jim, who was standing with all the superiority of a thirteen-year-old watching his sister at work.

Foster took off the rucksack to adjust the straps. The empty bag was annoying him.

'Dad.' The voice was uncertain.

'Dad. You'd better come. There's someone here.' The boy was backing away from where the dog's tail could be seen sticking up among the heather.

2

The valley was well into shadow as A. N. Drew, known behind his back as 'Drew-Drew', completed his examination of the site. He nodded to the policemen who were waiting.

'That's it,' he said. 'Nothing much else to do tonight. We'll just cover things over. The body can go now.' He stood off to one side and started to button up his light brown raincoat.

'It's getting chilly,' he said to his assistant, who was putting a camera into a small case beside plastic bags with various objects in them, each neatly tagged with a note of its contents. A larger case was at his feet.

'Right, lads,' said Inspector Paget in a military tone of voice.

Two of the three constables came forward with a collapsible stretcher. The third, an older man, spread a canvas sheet over the body, and wrapped it around it. The two carefully lifted the body on to the stretcher. Drew's assistant came forward with a shotgun in a long plastic bag. He laid it on the stretcher beside the body. The third constable shouldered a gamekeeper's bag, which had been lying to one side. Then the stretcher party set off, led by the third constable who picked out the easiest route for them.

'Have you ever observed,' said Drew to Paget as they watched them go on their way, 'that in a field the cow tracks always take the lines of least resistance while maximizing elevation gain and loss?'

'Can't say I have,' said Paget politely.

'Your men aren't going the easiest way,' said Drew.

'If that means that my constables aren't cows, thank you,' said Paget.

'It might mean they have less sense than cows,' said the assistant quietly to himself.

Drew, who heard him, smiled. Paget pretended that he did not, but his lips twitched too.

'Bert. What's ado with Paget?' asked the constable at the rear of the small procession as they got out of earshot of the Inspector and Police Surgeon.

'I don't know,' said the one at the head end. 'I've never seen him like that. Mind you, I felt quite queer myself, seeing this.' He gave a slight joggle to the stretcher.

'Don't,' said the other. 'It's bad enough without you doing a jig.'

At length they came to a more level part of the path, and by mutual consent they paused for a rest. Then it was on to the crest of the hill, to beside the Fosters' 'Stonehenge' where again they paused, this time for a longer rest.

They stood, looking down into the valley which was rapidly turning blue as the evening shadows swiftly darkened.

'Funny place,' said the youngest, shaking his head. 'It's quite nice, and yet . . .'

One of his fellows grunted. The eldest took out cigarettes.

'Thanks, Corky,' said the youngest, taking one.

There were footsteps on the path behind them.

'Ah, the Constabulary,' said a forcedly jovial voice. 'My journey is not in vain.' The figure was short, and somewhat out of breath.

'Oh, it's you,' said Corky curtly.

'Come now. Come now,' said the newcomer, airily. 'The Gentlemen of the Press have a right to know what is going on.'

'How did you get here?' asked the constable.

'We have our sources of information,' said the other smoothly. 'Where was it?' He tapped the stretcher with a negligent foot.

'Stop that,' said Corky, spokesman by reason of being oldest. 'Show some respect, man!'

The reporter paid little attention, his eyes darting about. Then he caught sight of the light raincoat down at the spring.

'Down there, was it?'

'Please yourself,' said Corky. 'Come on, lads.'

Without a further word the two lifted the stretcher and set off down the other side of the hill. The police ambulance showed palely down in the lay-by from which Foster and his family had started happily those few hours before. It looked a long way away.

The reporter watched them tramp along for a short distance, then he turned to go down to the three figures in the valley. Somehow, without an audience, he seemed to have lost his bounce. It was a suddenly old man that trudged his way down, oblivious of the scenery, his eyes on where he was putting his feet, and there alone. One could feel sorry for him.

'I could hit that fellow,' said Corky, tramping firmly forward.

'Me too,' said the second. 'I hope I catch him doing something sometime. Even a parking ticket would be a pleasure.'

'He is a right cur,' said Corky. 'They're not all like that, but he is a right one. Something funny about him too. All those airs and graces.' He snorted. 'Gentlemen of the Press. Puke him.'

'I heard he was once a reporter down in London,' said the youngest constable as he stumbled his way along.

'So they say,' said the oldest.

'It's true,' interjected Bert, who was now carrying the legs end of the stretcher. 'My brother-in-law's brother is down in London. He's a printer. Was with *The Times* till the fuss, and now he's got a job with a book printing firm. We were down there for holidays last year and he asked about a Henry Irwin. Couldn't be our one, I said. But it could.'

'What was he saying about him?'

'Nothing much. He had been a good reporter, but something went wrong. Wife trouble I think was the rumour, and he had dropped out of sight. Someone had thought he had come up this way.'

'It's a pity he can't be civil,' said the youngest, thoughtfully. 'He writes well.'

'Oh, I'll give you that,' said the oldest.

'What was the wife trouble?' asked the youngest.

'Oh, you and your fixations,' said Bert. 'Just wait till you're married and settled. That'll cool your imaginations.' He gave the stretcher a tug.

'Look out,' said the youngest. 'You almost made me let go.'

They marched on in silence for a while. Then conversation resumed.

'I think the wife ran out on him, and took the child. And I think the courts left her with the child too,' said Bert.

'Ah,' said the eldest sagely. 'That might explain a lot.'

'How?' asked the youngest.

'Well,' said the oldest, 'I've noticed that he is always kind to folk who've got that kind of thing in their background— it sometimes comes out reading like a plea in mitigation, almost. And he's always got a sweetie or something for a youngster. Maybe there's something there.'

'He's still a tube,' said the youngest.

Bert laughed.

'Eh?' said Corky.

'Fancy coming back up here tonight to carry him down?' said the other.

'That would be a mountain rescue job,' said the youngest.

'Not if Paget does him in. He can't stand Irwin, and he was in a funny mood back there. What was wrong with him? I never got an answer. I asked miles back.'

'I think he knew the deceased,' replied the eldest.

That silenced his companions, and they made their way solemnly down the two or three hundred feet or so to the ambulance.

Irwin did not look well by the time he made it down to where the three figures were preparing to leave. White tape roughly outlined a rectangle in the heather.

'What's going on?' he puffed as he arrived. But without waiting for the reply he stood balancing awkwardly on one foot, and tugged off the other shoe. Trying to empty it of bits of heather and small pebbles, he lost his balance and had to put the foot down. 'Blast,' he said as the sock swiftly absorbed wet from the moss he stood on.

Paget looked at him with distaste, and said nothing.

'Come now,' said Irwin, as he forced his shoe back on. 'I saw the body up there.' He jerked his head back to the skyline above them.

The corners of Paget's mouth turned down. 'A body has been found, and inquiries are proceeding,' he said.

'That all?' said Irwin in a sceptical tone. 'If it were as simple as that, why is Drew-Drew—sorry, Dr Drew—why is Dr Drew here?'

'That is all I have to say at this moment,' said Paget. 'If you want further details I suggest you talk to my superiors.'

'Are you going to add anything?' asked Irwin, swinging round on Drew, who had started to move off, carrying the small case.

'Inspector Paget has told you what can be said at this stage,' said Drew, and continued on his way.

'I don't suppose you have anything to say?' said Irwin to Drew's assistant.

'No, sir,' he replied, and picked up the heavier case and followed Drew.

'Are you coming too?' asked Paget.

Irwin looked around. 'Nothing much here, is there,' he said carelessly.

'Quite so,' said Paget. 'I cannot order you away, but there is nothing here, and I would remind you not to go inside the tape.'

Irwin smiled at that.

'Aren't we formal, old pal,' he said. 'I know my job as well as you know yours. And I know you. There's something afoot here. I can smell it.'

'I must go now,' said Paget. 'Coming?'

'All right,' said Irwin. 'Not too fast, though. I'm not as fit as I was, and these shoes aren't the best for hill-walking.'

The four stopped to catch their breaths where the constables had done so, and like them just stood in silence. At 'Stonehenge' they also stopped. Below them the valley was dark, the site of their labours quite indistinguishable in the gloaming.

Irwin sighed. 'Come on, fellows,' he said cajolingly. 'Can't you at least give me a "cause of death"?'

'That would be premature,' said Paget. 'The police will issue a statement in due course.' But, so saying, he eyed Irwin, who was glistening with sweat despite the chill of evening. He had somehow a beaten sort of look. Paget suddenly found himself sorry for him. What lay behind that reporter mask? What explained that listless look after Irwin had come all that way. There must be something. He took off his cap, and nodded to Drew. 'I dare say that you might get an educated guess, so long as you don't quote us.'

Drew smiled faintly. He too knew that public relations were important, and that rules were made to be bent in appropriate cases.

'Gunshot,' he said abruptly.

'Accident?' asked Irwin.

Drew said nothing.

'Come on,' said Paget. 'Time we were going.'

'Now look,' said Irwin, 'you can't just leave me like that. You haven't denied that it was murder, or suicide or anything.'

Drew set off down the path to the lay-by.

Irwin caught Paget's arm.

'Harry,' said Paget gently, 'you are a right pest. I should have said nothing at all. But I'll tell the folk back at the station to give you the story first.'

Irwin looked at him. There was something akin to pity in Paget's eyes.

'I don't want charity,' he said forcefully. 'I'm a good reporter. A good reporter. Why do you think I'm here?'

'I was wondering that,' said Paget.

'My God,' said Irwin. 'Do you want a statement?'

'We will,' said Paget.

'Why?'

'It is very strange. A body is found on the hills, somewhat remote from the usual paths that people take, and a reporter turns up. I don't think anything went out on the radio about it, though I know you folk monitor the police bands. Yet here you are.'

'I was passing,' said Irwin. 'I saw the ambulance in the lay-by and thought I should find out what was going on.'

'Very likely,' said Paget placidly. 'That will satisfy my bosses no doubt.'

'But that means that you are on an inquiry, and that probably rules out suicide, and Drew-Drew said it was a gunshot.'

'Come on,' said Paget, moving off.

Irwin followed.

When they were nearly back to the lay-by he came up to walk beside Paget.

'I don't suppose you know who it was?' he asked.

Paget walked on, lips pursed.

Irwin dodged in front of him so as to see his face.

'You do know,' he said triumphantly, seeing the expression on the face.

Paget nodded. He stopped.

'Yes,' he said heavily. 'I do know who it was. But I'm not telling you. You'll need to wait until the formalities have been completed.'

Irwin scrutinized his face. Then capitulated. He would settle for the best he could get, and that was not much.

'You'll make sure I get the story first,' he said rather than asked.

Paget resumed his walk, and Irwin fell in beside him.

'You'll get the story first,' Paget said. 'You can get it down to London or wherever else you want it to go. Much good may it do you.'

'You're very bitter.'

'I wonder,' replied Paget. 'I wonder.' He stopped and waved an arm at the surrounding countryside. Below them a car sped along the main road, its headlights on.

Irwin waited.

'I wonder,' said Paget in tones of finality, and started off walking again.

Down at the cars Drew and his assistant were waiting for them. Paget unlocked his car and Drew and his assistant got in. Irwin was on the point of saying something, but Paget merely shook his head as if sorrowfully.

'I'll phone in,' said Irwin.

'All right,' said Paget.

3

Early on the Monday morning, Mason drove up the estate road to Sunnyside Cottage. Crawford would arrive shortly, but he wanted to have a look at the dead man's accommodation on his own. Not a few times in the past something about the rooms occupied by a victim had given him a lead.

The dew was still lying on the grass as he parked, although it was a fine morning. There was an edge in the wind as it came down the valley behind the cottage. Sunnyside Cottage, indeed, he thought. That was wishful thinking. An advertising 'economy with the truth'. Some crows were calling in the trees down beside the river. Or were they ravens? He tried to recall the ancient verse. A single raven is a crow and a flock of crows are ravens—or is it the other way round? He shook his head. So much for his memory.

He took the keys from his pocket and went towards the door of the cottage. To its right a pile of branches and what looked like off-cuts from the sawmill on the other side of the village lay untidily against the wall. He skirted the pile, jingling the keys as he walked. Though he had had a search warrant in his pocket, the estate office had made no objection to letting him have the keys. The local football team was taking up all their attention: the violent death of one of their employees seemed to be a matter of less concern. Indeed, the man who had handed over the keys had positively grinned.

'Here you are,' he had said. 'Pity. I would have liked myself to see what went on in there. But . . .' He had shrugged and tossed Mason the keys.

Mason opened the door and went in. The house was gloomy and cold. He switched on the lights.

The living-room was a muddle. Untidy. Chaotic. The grate in the fireplace was full of wood ash. Beside the chair at one side of the fire was a stack of plastic-covered lager cans with discarded plastic and cardboard bases beside it. The top layer of the plastic had been ripped open and some cans were missing. They were probably among the pile at the other side of the fire. Briefly Mason had a vision of Hughes sitting beside a roaring fire, contentedly listening to his compact disc player or watching television, supping his way through the lager and throwing the cans idly in front of him.

He went over to the bookcases and examined them. Here there was some order but not much.

He went through to the kitchen. The remains of breakfast were on the table, and the sink was full of dishes. Mason stopped and worked out what was there. There were too many dishes for one person. He pursed his lips and went back into the living-room. The roll-top bureau was full of papers in no sort of order, seeming rather to have been stuffed into whatever space was available. In one of the divisions at the back of the writing surface he came across some bank statements. Four were recent. Mason was intrigued to find that Hughes had a healthy bank balance, with income from two sources coming in monthly by the looks of things. Well: that would explain how Hughes could afford the electronics that were sitting in the glossy cabinet beside the fireside chair. There seemed to be nothing else of interest.

As he turned from the desk, a glint of light caught his attention. On the floor against the wall beside the fireside chair were some letters under a piece of mica schist. He picked them up.

They were a mixture. A birthday card from someone called Joan, a reminder for a subscription to an estates magazine, and assorted pieces of junk mail. There was a letter from Wade and Company to do with an action being raised for child support. There was also a short, indeed curt, letter from a firm of London solicitors informing Hughes that they were not at liberty to discuss with him the matter which he had raised. Mason's broken eyebrow lifted. It lifted higher as he perused the letter at the bottom of the pile. On pink paper, it was clearly written in a female hand. He folded it and the solicitor's letter and put them in his inside pocket. The junk mail he left, carefully replacing the schist on top.

Upstairs was also a mess. The man had been a pig. There was no other word for it. Clothes lay all around the tangled bed. Mason shook his head and went back downstairs to take his leave. Then he thought he might as well make use of the facilities, and went into what he expected was the bathroom. It was merely a toilet. Glass scrunched under his feet as he went in. Someone had broken the window.

Carefully he shut the door and left. If someone had entered the cottage he wanted to find out who and why. Drew-Drew might manage to get something.

4

In the late morning Mason returned to the cottage with
Drew-Drew and his assistant. He parked where he had that
morning and led the way round the side of the cottage.
Grass grew right up to the cottage wall. A stunted bush or
two and some bramble tangles showed where there might
have been a garden. A discarded length of wood, clearly one
of the off-cuts from the pile at the front door, lay beneath
the broken window. Drew looked at it and frowned.

'Nothing to be got there,' he said, 'unless whoever did it
got his hand full of splinters.'

He surveyed the scene. Then he walked out into the
might-have-been garden and looked at the cottage. Mason
and the assistant waited for him. Drew looked at the bushes.

He came back.

'No. Nothing there,' he said. 'The deer must have been
down last night, but that's all. All right, Alistair. See what
you can get from the window and frame. I'll go inside.'

Mason and Drew walked back to the front door, leaving
the assistant to dust the window-frame.

At the front door Drew looked around.

'Pretty bleak,' he said.

'Very.'

Mason opened the door and let Drew in.

5

In the late afternoon Mason got up from his desk in Greyhavens Police Headquarters and went across to the window.
Below him the car park was full. Through the gap between

the wing of the building he was in and the block at the other
side of the car park he could see traffic moving on the main
road; the evening rush-hour traffic was building up. Briefly
he regretted his transfer from Birley, though it was good to
be back on home ground. He looked at his watch: 4.45. He
should be starting to pack up if he was going to be in time
to meet Jane's train.

He went back to his desk and once more flicked through
the thin file that lay on it. The name 'Evan Hughes' was
printed in rough pencil on the outside. He would have to
remember to get a properly typed label on the file before his
immediate boss saw it. Unlike the real 'Boss', he was one
of those who had risen by attention to such minutiæ as the
proper format for reports—but without great regard to the
content of the file.

The content of this one was thin. 'Evan Hughes': gamekeeper. Residence: Sunnyside Cottage, PenIron Estate.
Police Record: three convictions for drunkenness and brawl-
ing. Known to the Force as an occasional drunk but usually
harmless although belligerent. He wondered what Williams
might be able to add to all that—it might be handy knowing
someone local in this case, although it could also be a
nuisance. Body found by a family out on a Sunday ramble.
He shook his head. That must have been a shock.

Drew-Drew's report was a model of succinctness and lack
of technicality. Cause of death: gunshot from a shotgun, not
a handgun. A hole had been blown in the man's lower chest
and abdomen. The size of the major wound and the limited
distribution of pellets indicated that the assailant had been
close to the deceased, though there had been some balling
of the shot as well, increasing its destructive impact. Death
had probably been instantaneous because of the massive
drop in blood pressure caused by the wound and severance
of major arteries.

He turned to the photographs once more. They were
well done. The body lay surrounded by heather, as Paget

described. That man Foster had been more imprecise. He had thought it lay in a clump of heather, but the other photographs showed there was a sheep track through the heather at that point. He looked at the close-ups. The one in the heather showed Hughes with a slight sneer on his face; though that might just be the angle at which the beaky nose was raised. In the mortuary the edges of the mouth had turned up. Perhaps the jogging of the stretcher, he thought. Or maybe the deceased was amused by the stir that his death had caused. He had always enjoyed wasting police time. But the photos were good. So often the mortuary photos were over-exposed, but Drew's new assistant had certainly mastered the techniques.

He got up and went to the window once again. The traffic was slowing. He had better get moving just in case he were caught. He wondered what Jane's reaction would be. For once he had remembered their anniversary before her mother's card had dropped on the mat that morning. Unconsciously his hand went to his wallet where the theatre tickets lay. He hoped she would be pleased. Perhaps it also would help with the news that he would have to go down to PenIron for a few days.

He put the Hughes file in the cabinet, locked it and got his coat.

He was just on his way down the stairs when he met Inspector Paget coming up.

'I wonder if I might have a word,' said Paget.

Mason stopped.

'In private,' said Paget apologetically, looking at the stream of typists and others around.

Mason shrugged and led the way back up the few steps to his room.

'It's just that I promised that we would give the Hughes story to Irwin,' said Paget as they entered Mason's room. 'I wondered if there was going to be a statement.'

'Yes,' said Mason. 'There is. Jessica is just typing it and

it was going on general release as soon as she was finished.'

He looked at Paget. 'I thought you didn't like the man.'

'I don't, or at least I didn't. But I felt sorry for him. There was something so hang-dog about him, and he did actually get all the way to the scene on just a hunch. And he did promise not to spring the story until there was a statement.'

'All right. Get the copy from Jessica and tell her to hold it for another half an hour. That'll give Irwin time to get it on the tapes if he is really serious. But don't hunt him out. If he hasn't come in by, say, six, let the thing go.' He smiled. 'We too have a duty to the media, you know.'

'Yes, sir,' said Paget. 'Actually he is downstairs just now, waiting.'

'Is he now?' said Mason. 'That's unusual. I would expect Mr Irwin to be waiting for the next round in the Golden Boy at this time in the afternoon.'

Paget nodded.

'We'll maybe have to get him to give a statement too.'

'I'll deal with that.'

'Tomorrow will do. Don't spoil his evening.'

'All right.'

Paget hesitated.

'Yes?' said Mason.

'I was just thinking . . . at least, it's none of my business, I know . . .'

'Yes? Go on, man.' Mason looked at his watch.

'It's just that Hughes must have known whoever shot him. Otherwise he could not have got so close to someone as that. It was a close-range wound.'

Mason smiled. 'Maybe we should transfer you to the detective branch,' he said kindly. 'That's very true. It is hard to think of someone just standing there waiting to be shot, particularly someone like Hughes.

Paget nodded, satisfied.

'Do you reckon that it was one of the local poachers, then?' asked Mason.

Paget pulled at his ear.

'Can't say I do,' he replied. 'I know you've got out instructions to pull in everyone who's been poaching with a gun, but I don't think it's any of those. Not, at least, any that we know of. Some of them are tough, but none of them are that tough. Not up here. London, perhaps, but not up here.' The last phrase sounded like an article of belief.

Mason shrugged. 'It's just that the Hughes we know would have been well-known to anyone who was going to go into his territory. They might well have taken the protection of a gun with them.'

'But all our gun-men go in with rifles. It's deer they are after, not rabbits. Not that far into the hills.'

Mason nodded. Paget had a good point.

'Still,' he said. 'Get them all in and get statements off all of them. Then we'll see what's there, if anything. My old teacher used to say that the police don't catch criminals by taking thought. They catch them by taking statements.'

Paget smiled politely. Mason had passed on that thought before.

6

The train was up to time. Mason stood at the end of the platform waiting to see where the small form of his wife would appear.

She was about half way down the train. As Mason walked towards her a figure got off behind her, and took her case. It was Peter Wade.

'Hello, Mr Wade,' said Mason formally, holding out his hand for the case.

'Here you are, Superintendent,' said Wade, handing it over.

'Good trip?' said Mason to Jane as the three of them walked across the concourse.

'Yes. Very good.'

'I thought you always flew,' he said to Wade.

'Usually,' said Wade. 'But this trip was arranged quickly on Thursday and there were no seats on suitable planes coming back. So I thought I would come up by train and use the time to go over some other material on the way.'

'Instead of which Mr Wade ended up talking to me for much of the way,' interjected Jane.

'Seven hours twenty-seven minutes?' said Mason in mock horror.

'I forgot your interest in trains,' said Wade.

Outside the station, Wade turned to the taxi-rank.

'Can we give you a lift?' asked Mason.

'No. It's too far. I've to collect my own car at the airport.'

Mason let him go.

Jane came close. She fitted neatly in below his chin.

'Miss me?' she asked.

'Of course. So much so that I've got a surprise.'

She tilted her head.

'Theatre tickets.'

She laughed. 'Don't tell me. Mother got on the phone last night.'

'Scout's honour. It was my own idea and I got them on Friday. You can see the credit-card statement when it comes in.'

'Phooey. That just gives the date they get the chit.'

'Now who's the detective?' He gave her a hug. 'And in any event I meant you can see the top copy that I get. It came in with the tickets in the post.'

'Well, we had better rush. I'll need to change.'

'And how is he?'

'Not bad. The accommodation is all right, and the landlady seems a nice kindly person. But I think he will be a bit homesick shortly. He's just realizing that he has flown the coop, and that it'll never be the same again.'

Mason nodded. He understood what she wasn't saying. He too felt keenly the gap now that their eldest was away. Still, now that Jane had seen him in his new place, she would be more content about it. The job was too good to have passed up.

7

The theatre was fun. That three local men could take the theatre for four weeks and fill it nightly said something about them and about the city. His sides were sore with laughter as they made their way home later that night.

'I was thinking about Paget during that song,' said Jane sleepily from her seat in the car.

'What song?'

'The one about the Prince of Wales.'

'There wasn't one about him.'

'Yes, there was. The one with the line about there being many men in the valley who looked like Edward.'

'Oh, that Prince of Wales. Yes?'

'Is it true?'

'They say so. There were several of Edward's bastards who were "adopted" up the valley.'

'But didn't adoption only start later than that?'

'Yes. I suppose that's true. I think adoption wasn't legal until the nineteen-thirties. But there were informal arrangements before that, and certainly for that sort of thing. Half the titled families start off as bastards.'

'Bar sinister,' said Jane, sitting up.

'What?'

'That's what shows bastardy in the coat of arms.'

'Where on earth did you get that information?'

'It's the title of some book or other I was reading.'

'So?'

'Well, next time you are talking to Paget, compare him with the statue of Edward at the corner of the Terrace gardens.'

Mason thought of the burly, grizzled inspector, and started to laugh.

'Careful,' said Jane. 'It wouldn't do for you to be taken up for careless driving.'

'He does come from up the valley,' said Mason reflectively.

Jane giggled.

8

The next afternoon, the Tuesday, Mason rang the bell at the PenIron Manse. Ann came to the door.

'Oh, come in,' she said, opening it wide.

Mason came in, brushing the light rain off his coat.

'I'm afraid Ted isn't in just now. He has been called to Hill House. It seems Miss Anthony has taken a shock,' she said. 'But come you through to the kitchen and have a mug of coffee. The kettle is on.'

They went through to the kitchen. Paul was perched at one end of the kitchen table, doing his homework. He made to collect it and leave, but his mother stopped him, saying that the two of them would be going through to the lounge just as soon as the kettle had boiled.

'How are you getting on, young Paul?' said Mason.

'Fine,' said the boy, easily evading an attempt to ruffle his hair.

'And how is Eric?' asked Ann. 'Wasn't Jane coming back yesterday from seeing him.'

'He's fine. Jane got back yesterday. He seems to have settled down well, though there was a bout or two of home-

sickness in the first week or so. It's his first time away from
home on his own.'

Ann nodded. 'I remember what it was like when I first
realized that I had flown the coop,' she said. She looked
anxiously at her own eldest.

Mason followed her gaze, and smiled.

'It comes to us all,' he said. 'Enjoy them while you have
them.'

The kettle clicked off.

Ann was just pouring the second mug when Williams
came in.

'Hello, Alan,' he said. 'I thought I recognized the car.'
Then he turned to Ann. 'That for me?' he asked, picking up
one of the mugs.

'It's mine,' said Mason, taking it from him.

'Oh, well. Then this one is mine,' said Williams, picking
up the other.

Ann firmly took it from him. 'You know where they are
kept,' she said, and shepherded Mason through to the
lounge.

She looked up, her eyes full of fun, when Williams came
into the lounge with his own mug steaming in his hand.
But she read something in his expression, and sobered
quickly.

'What is it?' she asked.

'I am afraid Miss Anthony has passed away,' said
Williams slowly.

'Oh, Ted!' said Ann.

'That's the old lady you were visiting?' asked Mason.

'Yes,' said Williams heavily. He sat down beside Ann on
the settee and leaned forward to put his mug down on an
occasional table.

'How old was she?' asked Mason.

'I'm not sure,' said Williams. 'I dare say all that will
come out in due course, but I just don't know exactly.'

'Relatives?' asked Mason.

'None,' said Williams. 'It was her nephew, her only nephew, that Peter Wade shot last August. You remember.' He looked directly, almost challengingly, at Mason.

'Yes. Of course. Stupid of me not to make the connection,' said Mason.

The three sat in silence for a minute or so.

Ann sipped at her coffee, shoulders hunched, holding the mug as if it were a bowl in her hands.

At length Williams also began to drink. Mason continued merely to hold his mug, his face blank.

'What brings you here?' asked Williams.

'I've been assigned to deal with this Hughes business,' said Mason, taking a swig of his drink.

'Ah yes. Sounds nasty, that,' said Williams. 'It was all over the *Greyhavens Gazette*.'

Mason nodded. 'We're going to have to have the incident caravan down here for a few days and do a house to house round the village,' he said.

'Why?' asked Ann. 'He was killed away up one of the glens, almost across to the north road.'

'I know,' said Mason. 'But he was local to this area, and the valleys lead out this way. We have to ask around, and there isn't anyone living over on the other side of the Grey Hill.'

Out of the corner of his eye he saw Williams shudder. He turned to him.

'He took me over there last August. Just after the shooting,' said Williams. 'He took me stalking. Right over the top of the shoulder. There was a herd close by down in the valley. It was wonderful.' He stopped.

Mason watched him.

'He had a bad reputation,' said Ann. 'Girls and drink.'

'Do you think he had enemies?' said Mason quietly.

'Oh yes,' said Ann.

'Ann,' said Williams reproachfully.

She turned to him. 'Well, he had,' she said. She turned

back to Mason. 'There were a few who would have been glad to see him go. He had been a cuckoo in a few nests.'

'Ann!' said Williams, more forcefully.

'It's true.' She relaxed into her chair. 'But I suppose we shouldn't speak ill of the dead.'

Mason smiled.

'Are you visiting us professionally?' Ann asked.

'Not really,' said Mason. 'Or I should say, not at first. Or not first and foremost. But when you say things like that about someone who has been gunned down, and I am in charge of the investigation, you cannot expect me to pay no attention, now can you?'

Ann's smile conceded the point.

'Can you tell me anything about the man?' asked Mason.

'Not much,' said Williams. 'He lived in the parish so I visited him, naturally, when we came here first, and I have been back several times.'

'Was he a member of your congregation?'

'No.'

'Then, why?' Mason gestured expressively.

'He invited me to come back the first time I went, and I suppose I thought it showed some interest in the affairs of the Kingdom.'

'Did it?'

'Not yet.' Williams corrected himself. 'At least, he used to say the odd thing which indicated that he had been thinking on those lines, and I suppose I hoped to encourage that.'

'A brand snatched from the burning?'

'Something like that.'

'So what did you think of him?'

'Well, he had a terrible reputation for drink, and for pursuing women. The last time I was at his house was when he invited me on that stalking trip, and I remember thinking then that I heard a woman's voice upstairs while I was waiting for him. But he was an odd fellow as well. He was

curiously well—and curiously ill-informed. Have you been
to his house?'

Mason shrugged noncommittally.

'Well, you will see what I mean by that when you go—
you will be going, I take it?'

Mason did not reply. He wondered what his friend had
seen.

'The main room downstairs is the only one I have been
in, apart from the kitchen. The kitchen would make you
vomit. And the room is not much better. There's stacks of
books on all the walls and a right odd collection it is. I got
a chance to have a look last time, and there were good old
books and modern rubbish all higgledy-piggledy. Some
Solzhenitsyn next to crime novels, a group of occultist trash
. . . go and see.'

'Umm. Anything else?'

Williams thought, and Ann spoke up from the shelter of
his arm.

'You said to me that he had a good knowledge of music.'

'So I did,' said Williams. 'Yes. That is an oddity. You'll
see that he has rather an expensive-looking music centre,
and I think a compact disc player as part of it. It seems
strange to me, but Hughes knew a lot about decent music.'

Mason laughed. 'Knowing you, I assume that "decent"
means Mozart and Beethoven.'

Williams smiled. 'And Shostakovich and Bruckner. That
was the surprising thing. To find a gamekeeper who had
solid opinions on such composers, and on the relative merits
of Haitink or Kubelik or Bruckner. Most odd.'

'You intrigue me,' said Mason. 'There does seem to be
more here than meets the eye. We—the police, that is—
have already heard something of his womanizing record,
and of course we know him for his drink. His name has
come up quite often in the court news. But what you say
sounds very strange.'

'I think he was self-educated,' said Mason. 'I thought

once from something he said that he had been a University drop-out in the 1960s, when it was fashionable.'

'A hippie,' said Ann delightedly.

'Exactly,' said Williams. 'But he set me right about that. He had a down on that sort of education.'

'That doesn't mean he never was there himself. In fact it could point the other way,' observed Mason.

'True,' said Williams. 'But he did tell me once that he had spent all his life in gamekeeping and that sort of work, first down in Wales where he grew up, and then he came straight here from there. No. He educated himself in what interested him. He is—was—one of those voracious readers, omnivores, and carried it over to his interest in music.' He turned to Ann. 'Remember that night I came home and told you about "The Rite of Spring"?'

She laughed. Mason raised a polite eyebrow.

'It was in the days before he had got that music centre, and he was using mainly cassettes in rather a nice big Hitachi player,' went on Williams. 'I went there and we got on to the topic of music and how different performances can bring out different things. Well, he grubbed about and produced, I forget how many recordings of "The Rite of Spring"— Stravinsky, you know. There must have been ten or eleven, some pre-recorded and some off BBC concerts.'

Mason nodded.

'Well, he made me listen to most of them. Not all of it— that might have been a pleasure hearing it three or four times by different good orchestras and conductors. But no. He wanted me to hear how each did that sort of rush up to the break at the middle, and then the final dance.'

'On cassette?' asked Mason, incredulously.

'Precisely,' said Williams. 'It was appalling. He fiddled with it running each one forward and back with only a snatch or two of the music to guide him. He certainly seemed to know the music. He needed only three or four notes to work out where it was on the tape. But the performances were all different in length, because the conductors all took different speeds. And some of the tapes were C60s and some were C90s, so he couldn't estimate properly and use the rev counter. It was just amazing. And he was so enthusiastic. And so truculent when I tried either to help, or to suggest that I had got the point.'

'Yes,' said Mason. 'I gather he could get very upset.'

'What I don't understand,' said Ann, 'is where he got the money from. Apparently he was always complaining about the wages that Miss Anthony paid him.'

'That's true,' said Williams.

Mason shifted in his seat, but said nothing.

'Yes,' Williams went on, 'he always let it be well known that he was paid scandalously low wages. But he seemed to live as well as he wanted to.'

'And had money for drink,' said Mason wryly.

'Indeed.'

'I wonder what put him on to music,' Mason mused.

'The Third Programme,' Williams suggested.

'You mean Radio Three,' Ann corrected him.

'Ah yes,' said Mason. 'Our egalitarian labelling again.' He got to his feet. 'I'd better be going. I was only passing.'

'Are you to be down here for long?' asked Ann. 'Are you travelling up and down, or can we give you a bed.'

'Thanks,' said Mason. 'That is kind of you. But I am down with some others and I think it would be better for good relations if I go to the hotel like them.'

'Well you can always come here and play trains in the evening,' said Ann with a grin.

'Is that heresy, or blasphemy?' Mason queried.

'Both,' said Williams, catching his wife in a firm grip.

'How long will you be down?' said Ann.

'I'm not sure yet. It will depend what we get out of our visiting.'

'Well you will at least come and have a meal.'

'No, I think it would be better if I did not do that.'

'How many of you are there?' asked Ann. 'We could take several of you.'

Mason smiled. 'It's not that. It just might be better if the police were not seen around your manse too often in the next few days.'

'Oh,' said Ann. Then more slowly, 'Yes. Of course. I see.'

'I am sorry,' said Mason. 'You cook like a dream. Almost as good as Jane. So much so that I feel guilty in not letting my people have the chance to have one of your meals. But we are down on a professional matter.'

'It's all right,' said Williams. 'We understand. You are quite right. It may be difficult enough these next few days without having the Constabulary too much in evidence.'

Mason nodded. 'Well, I had better be on my way. I may come back and ask some more about Hughes in due course. But don't worry, Ted. I'll not ask you to break any confessional—at least not yet.'

'I hadn't thought of that,' said Williams soberly. 'It would be awful if whoever did it came to me and confessed.'

'He's in favour of capital punishment,' confided Ann.

'I know,' said Mason.

Williams ventured a slight smile. 'Well, if you are having difficulty with—what was it Poirot called them? your little grey cells?—if you are having trouble, you can come and try the therapeutic effect of careful manual labour. I am needing to get something like fifty or sixty North British trucks painted in the next week or so. You could fill in an evening or so on that. And get my thanks into the bargain.'

'We'll see,' said Mason.

'It's not got anything to do with Wade's accident?' said Williams suddenly.

Mason paused. 'I had forgotten about that. We didn't get anywhere with that, did we?'

'Not that anyone down here heard about.'

Mason nodded. 'I'll need to think about that.'

9

That evening Mason gloomily perused Drew's report on Hughes's cottage. There was some blood on glass left in the window-frame. Inside, other than two indications of gloved fingers, there was nothing to help him. Drew had been verbally quite colourful in his reactions, but the report submitted excluded such comment bar one.

'In this case it is difficult to distinguish between the effects of a search and the prior arrangement of the contents of the room,' Drew had written. What he had said as he placed the sheet of paper on Mason's desk in the mobile incident room was that while Mason might care to arrest all persons found to have a cut finger in the area, the only real lead that Mason could look for was if someone had eaten something while searching the house. He suggested that Mason might check the local hospitals for admissions of persons suffering from botulism. Any such could well be prime suspects.

Mason kneaded his eyes. This one looked like being a long slow job. He had three constables assigned to him apart from his assistant Ian. It would not take them too long to go round the village and get a general set of notes together. Then they would see what they had.

He took out of his pocket the letters he had taken from the cottage and re-read them. Then he sat, looking out through the caravan window. The London solicitors would have to be contacted—that could be done in the morning. In the meantime, what about the letter from the woman. That could be dynamite in a village like this. Would he have to detonate it? He would wait for the reports of the visitation, and then see. Perhaps it would not be necessary.

He got up and left the caravan, locking it behind him. A

couple of children scuttled for cover as they saw him emerge. That hurt.

He went across to the PenIron Arms. The others would be there before they went out on the evening round. It would be cold work going round the houses where there had been no reply earlier in the day. But such routine was the only way to crack a nut like this one.

10

Later that evening he rang the bell at the manse. Ann let him in.

'I succumbed,' he said.

'I expected that. Ted is up at Toytown.'

Mason nodded, hung up his coat and went upstairs.

Williams was at the back of the room underneath the staging of the layout when Mason tapped at the door and went in.

'Good,' came Williams's voice. 'I've been having some trouble with the switching for the points system. Something is shorting intermittently and it's playing havoc with the siding system. Could you try the switches while I check things out over here.'

Mason sat down at the control panel and threw all the switches to 'off'.

'Idiot,' came Williams's voice again as various relays operated beside him. 'I'd already done some of that.'

'Do it again to double check.'

Williams snorted.

The two worked in virtual silence for a few minutes, punctuated only by Williams's 'Next.'

'What like a day has it been?' asked Williams at last.

'Raining, latterly.'

'Getting anywhere?'

'Difficult to say. About a third of the houses had no one in so the boys are going round those this evening.'

'Double checking?' Williams's tone was wry.

'Quite.'

'Next.'

'You were right. The place was a mess, and an odd mess at that.'

'Next.'

'Have you heard anything of Hughes being sued in respect of a baby?'

'Yes.'

'Are you pleading clergyman confidence?'

'No. Peter Wade told me that he was acting for the girl.'

'And who might she be?'

There was a pause.

'I can, of course, get that information from the court lists if the action has been filed.'

'Next.'

Mason waited.

'Next. It's Iris Maddon. She's just finishing school.'

'Anything else?'

'Not really. It has all been a shock. The matter came to my attention only last month at the church fair. Her father is an elder and he is on the financial Board as well.'

'Why at the fair?'

'Next. Well, if you really want to know there was a bust-up between Hughes and Maddon, or the other way round. Maddon assaulted Hughes and got pushed into the Cake and Candy stall for his pains.'

Mason remained still.

'Next . . . Ah. That seems to be the culprit.' Williams scrabbled about, came out from under the staging, rummaged in a tool-box for a pair of pliers and disappeared again.

'He must have been quite a brave man,' ventured Mason.

'Hughes was formidable.'

Williams re-emerged and stood up. He picked up a bit of towelling and started to clean his hands.

'Not so much brave as blazing angry, I believe.'

'Does he shoot?' asked Mason in a bland tone.

'Yes. Yes, he does. In fact he won the prize at the fair for shoo . . .' Williams's voice tailed off and he stopped cleaning his hands. 'Look here, you couldn't suspect Harry Maddon. He's an elder.'

Mason said nothing.

'No. Out of the question,' stated Williams firmly. 'Harry is basically a good man, even if a bit confused. There's no way he would have done it.'

'Would have or could have?'

'Would have.'

'Just because he's active in your church? I know one such man who is presently a guest of Her Majesty. He saw himself as an avenging angel.'

Williams looked at Mason strangely. 'I know about that one,' he said. 'He was in Ian Mackenzie's church. You're talking about the Ebony House business.'*

'Yes.'

'Well, this is not the same. I cannot think that there is anyone local involved.'

'How well do you know your parish?'

'Well enough.'

Mason shrugged. 'Tell me more about your Harry Maddon. It's not a name that has come up so far in our inquiries.'

Williams outlined what he knew. Maddon was a successful businessman. He had started as an accountant but had moved over into business administration and was the area manager for a national furniture firm. He travelled to each of the three main stores in his area once a week, and occasionally was away all night. Usually, however, he was home each night. He was a faithful member of the church,

---

* *A Death in Time.*

though his interest in sermons was limited.

'He's more your "blessed thought" calendar man,' concluded Williams with a smile.

'And the wife?'

'Mavis is devoted to him, and they are both devoted to their daughter. She's called Iris, and I would think that if she has kicked over the traces it may be because the parents would have been just too suffocating.'

'Does the daughter shoot?'

'Lord, no!' Williams looked carefully at Mason again. 'What sort of a mind have you got?'

'221b Baker Street. Exclude all the possibilities, and what is left is the truth even if it is impossible.'

'That's misquoted.'

Mason smiled. He turned to the railway layout. 'I see you have revised the spur line to the colliery.'

Williams accepted the change of subject with some relief, and the two of them spent the next hour or so on railway matters.

Ann came up with tea about half past nine.

'I may have a problem,' said Mason, accepting his mug.

She looked her question, as she perched on a high stool.

'It seems that Mr Hughes had sources of income other than his employment.'

'What does that mean?' asked Williams.

'Among the papers are bank statements. Every month he was getting a respectable sum from a bank in London.'

'Blackmail?' said Ann.

'I'm interested that you should say that,' replied Mason. 'It crossed my mind. Why should it cross yours?'

'Ann reads too many crime novels,' laughed Williams.

'I'm serious,' said Mason, disregarding him. 'Why did blackmail occur to you?'

Ann puckered her brow. 'I don't know. But it's the

usual explanation for unexplained payments when there is a murder involved, isn't it?'

'Ted's right. You do read too many crime novels. Blackmail is really very rare.'

Williams intervened. 'You mean that blackmail is not often detected. What about all the undetected blackmail that you don't know about?'

Mason shrugged. 'Let's leave that. If we were to assume that blackmail is involved, who would you suggest is paying the blackmail, and for what?'

'That's easy,' said Ann quickly. 'Peter Wade is paying Evan Hughes because that wasn't an accident last August, and Evan is—was—' she corrected herself, 'in a position to testify about it.'

There were two immediate reactions.

'Ann!' said Williams, banging his mug down on the track beside him so hard that it slopped over. He pulled out a handkerchief and began to daub at the tea. Ann watched tolerantly.

'There's a thought,' said Mason slowly, tensing and clearly juggling all sorts of ideas in his mind. Then he relaxed. 'No,' he said. 'It's an interesting idea as a motive, but then we would have to work out why Wade shot Harold Anthony and that was negatived when that shooting was looked into. It was an accident.'

There was a silence, which Mason broke.

'Besides, Wade was down in London this last weekend. He came back up on the train with Jane. I met them at the station.'

Ann laughed. 'Well, if that is the case then clearly Wade is your prime suspect. It is always the one with the best alibi who does it.'

Even Williams chuckled.

Mason got up, smiling. 'I know. Well, I had better be getting back to the hotel. Thanks for the shelter and for your help.' He shook a finger at Ann. 'If I want any more hairy ideas I'll know where to come.'

'Come in any case,' said Williams. 'I've still got those trucks to paint.'

11

On the Thursday morning Mason was in a grumpy mood. He hated a strange bed, and as a result had not slept well. He spent quite some time drafting and re-drafting a letter to the solicitors in London whose letter he had picked up from the floor of Hughes's cottage. His irritation at life kept breaking through into the wording. But eventually he settled for simplicity, stating that their letter had been found in the house of someone who had, it was thought, been murdered. He was in charge of the investigations and he wondered whether they could shed any light on the correspondence. He also wrote to the London bank whose statements he had picked up.

It was mid-morning before the reports of the previous night's additional visits were given to Mason.

'Took your time,' he growled at Paget as he delivered the file. 'Anything?'

'Nothing that seems obvious to any of us, sir,' said Paget. He too had had a bad night, and as he stood he rubbed his side.

'What's wrong with you?'

'I'm not sure, sir. I didn't sleep too well. I think the bed is a bit damp and it has gone for my fibrositis.'

Mason suddenly smiled, his eyebrow tilting as he did so.

'Why don't you say it? You think that I didn't have too good a night either, and wish I wouldn't take it out on you.'

Paget grinned.

'Off you go. There's still some visiting to be done.'

Once Paget had left, Mason looked through the notes. One in particular interested him greatly.

He got up and put on his coat against the freshness of the morning breeze.

12

The tyres scrunched on the gravel as he drew up on a wide parking area beside the buildings. He sat for a moment and looked around. The stables were well kept. In a small field to his right beyond a neat white fence was the usual apparatus of small jumps for beginners. Beyond it he could see several horses.

A girl came round the corner of the buildings, leading a fine-looking horse. She glanced at the car and then led the horse on through the archway into the stable yard. Mason followed.

'I'm looking for Mrs Robertson,' he said.

'She's in the house,' said the girl. 'Round the corner.'

Mason walked back and round. Probably it was not worth taking the car.

Round the corner lay a modern bungalow, looking out over the valley. There were two cars parked nose to tail on the path to the front door. As he walked up the path, the door burst open. A largish man came out.

'Please yourself,' he flung back over his shoulder to an attractive woman who had come into the doorway. 'Don't say I didn't warn you.'

He got into the rear-most car, and reversed back erratically. Mason had to jump to avoid being hit. Then, with flying grit, the car disappeared round the corner. Mason watched it go.

When he turned, the woman was watching him.

'I'm so sorry,' she said. 'My brother gets so angry. What can I do for you?'

'Mrs Robertson? Mrs Elizabeth Robertson?'

'Yes?'

'My name is Mason, Superintendent Mason. I am from the police.'

The woman's face went slack, and for a moment Mason saw her as she would be in future years. She put a bandaged hand up to her mouth. With her left she gripped the door-frame. Then she pulled herself together.

'Yes,' she said. 'Won't you come in?'

When they were settled in the front room with its picture window, Mrs Robertson sat very straight, her hands folded in her lap.

'Now, Superintendent, how may I help you?'

'Your brother usually drives like that?' Mason gestured vaguely towards the drive.

'Yes, I am afraid he does. He's in the garage business, but treats cars dreadfully. If I treated my horses the way he does cars . . .' She fluttered a hand.

'I'm sorry to see you have been injured,' said Mason.

'Oh, it's nothing. Nothing at all.'

'It does seem to have soaked the bandage. Did you take it in to Casualty in case you needed stitches?'

'No, no. It really is not that bad. I just bandaged it because of working with the horses, you know.'

'Barbed wire? Or a slipping can-opener? My wife cut herself quite badly only a month or so ago on a can.'

'Yes. Yes, it was a can. Careless.'

Mason looked out across the valley.

'Beautiful situation you have here.'

'Yes. Yes, indeed. When I was girl down in the village I used to dream of having a house up here. The old stables were falling into rack and ruin and the house was worse, but Keith was able to buy it and we did up the stables and built this bungalow in place of the old house.'

'Keith?'

'My husband. He works in Greyhavens.'

'Ah! I think I know of him.'

'Not professionally, I hope.'

'No.'

The woman sat even straighter. Mason was tempted to let the silence lengthen to see what might happen.

She fidgeted.

'I understand that one of the constables came round interviewing yesterday evening and spoke to both yourself and your husband.'

'Yes?'

'I hope he was courteous?'

'Yes. Yes, indeed he was. Very courteous, but he wouldn't have anything to drink. Which reminds me, would you like a cup of tea? It's about time I made one for Mary.'

'Mary?'

'Mary Begg. She's my stable-girl. Molly, the other one, has her day off today.'

Mason waited quietly while Mrs Robertson went through to the kitchen. He heard her calling to the girl. Shortly after that she came back with a tray, and put it on a small tea-table between them.

In the meantime she seemed to have gained in composure. As she poured the tea she said, 'Now. What was it that brought you all this way? Keith and I told the constable all that we could. He wanted to know where we were last weekend, and I told him. We were at the Perth sales. I bought two beautiful young colts. We didn't hear of the death until we came home on Monday evening.'

Mason looked at her, and she met his gaze with a challenge in her eyes.

'None the less you do not seem too surprised to see me this morning,' he said.

'I know you have to be very thorough. Presumably you have to go round everyone twice to see if there are any discrepancies.'

Mason shrugged. 'No. What you both said to my man last night was very full and no doubt we could check the information you have given us. I gather that your husband even offered to find the hotel bill. No. There's something else.'

She stiffened.

'I was wondering if you had ever been to Evan Hughes's cottage,' said Mason blandly.

'I beg your pardon?' There was ice in her voice.

'I was wondering if you had ever been to Evan Hughes's cottage,' repeated Mason smoothly.

'Never.' The tone was definite.

'Never?'

'Never. What would take me to his cottage?'

'I find myself wondering if you were there on Monday, or Sunday evening.'

She glanced at her bandaged hand.

'Yes,' sighed Mason. 'And there were horse droppings round the back where you tethered your horse to the bushes in the garden.'

She rose to her feet. 'This is ridiculous. I shall report you to your superiors.'

Mason took the pink letter from his inside pocket and laid it on his cup on the tea-table.

Mrs Robertson slowly sank back down on to her seat. She stared at the letter. Then she covered her face with her hands and began to cry.

Mason put the letter back in his pocket and waited.

She began to talk through her hands. The affair had been recent, short, and to her, surprising. She had met Hughes while exercising a horse on PenIron land which lay over the hill behind the stables. He had been there the next day, and the next.

'I'm so ashamed.' She looked up. 'But he was like a drug.'

Mason nodded.

'I had to get the letters back,' she went on.

'So when you heard he was dead, you went over on one of your horses. When?'

'Monday morning. I heard a rumour. It's not far if you go straight over the hill.'

'And broke the window in the toilet, and cut yourself.'

She nodded. 'I was so scared that Keith would get to know. I had to have the letters back.'

'Letters.'

'Letters. I thought I had them all.'

She stared gloomily at the table, then straightened again.

'But it was all over before that. He told me that I wasn't his type. I suppose he was right.'

'So you drove up from Perth, walked in from the road, because you knew he would be on the Grey Hill, and shot him.'

'No.' She was angry. 'Not at all. I told you we were in Perth over the weekend at the sales.'

'I see.'

Mason paused.

'Did anyone else know of your infatuation?'

'No.'

'Are you sure?'

'So far as I know.'

'Your husband didn't? Nor your brother?'

She blenched.

Mason rose. 'Well, I had better be going,' he said. 'I'll see myself out.'

As he went down the path he glanced back at the picture window. Betty Robertson was still sitting where he had left her.

13

Mason prided himself that he was in good physical condition. He thought that that meant that his reflexes were also tuned up, able to cope with any eventuality, and perhaps that was ordinarily the case. Nonetheless, he did not see the punch that sent him sprawling in the Milne Garage that afternoon.

Crawford, who had been off to one side, made to restrain Douglas Milne, but Mason intervened.

'Leave him, Ian. Leave him,' he said, and Crawford stopped, but remained watchfully close as Mason lay looking up at the large man.

'You say that again, and I'll beat you into a pulp.' Douglas Milne shook his fist at Mason, and, ignoring Crawford, turned and stamped out of the garage building.

Mason got up slowly. He dusted himself down.

'Why didn't we book him?' asked Crawford.

'It was partly my fault,' said Mason, with a smile. 'I was looking for a reaction, and I should have expected what I got.'

Crawford looked puzzled.

'I caught a sight of his temper this morning,' explained Mason enigmatically. 'Come on.'

Outside Milne was attending to a car at the petrol pumps. Mason and Crawford went into the kiosk on the garage forecourt. Mason sat down and waited. Crawford looked at the racks of sweets.

Milne came in. He ignored the two officers, wrote on a pad, got change from the till and went back out to the car. Then he went back into the garage.

After a minute, when it was clear Milne was not going to re-appear, Mason and Crawford followed him. There was a car up on the hydraulic jack. Milne was underneath it, pulling on goggles, a blow-torch in his hand.

'Look,' said Mason from a safe distance and deliberately not looking at the flame. 'You are going to have to talk with us sooner or later. If I wish I can have you brought to me, but I thought it better to talk here. Make up your mind.'

The acetylene flared blue. Mason looked the other way. A section of exhaust pipe clattered to the floor. Milne shut off the flame, and came out from under the car. He pointed to the door.

'Leave,' he said.

14

Back at the incident caravan there was an appearance of business at the three desks in the public area, but from experience Mason could tell that the atmosphere was missing. In the past he had felt an almost psychic charge building up when something was afoot, as though amid the routine the investigators could sense a successful conclusion to their efforts not far off. 'They're like a pack of hounds going out to scent on a good day,' his first boss had put it, and Mason knew what he had meant. But today was not one of those days. There was no tingle.

He went in to his private office. There were a pile of reports waiting, and he picked up the topmost and quickly skimmed through it. There was nothing there. Nor in the one beneath. At the foot of the pile was a note. There had been a phone call from a woman to headquarters back in Greyhavens asking for an interview. According to the message, she had indicated she had 'some information about the Hughes matter' which she would 'divulge only to the person in charge of the investigation', and that only in Greyhavens. The Boss had taken it upon himself to arrange the interview for the next day at 10.15, if that was convenient. Mason wrote 'OK' in large letters across the top of the note and circled them. It would be a good excuse not to spend another night down here in this Godforsaken spot. Then he chided himself. Williams would hardly consider it Godforsaken. It was his patch. Mason went out to the public area.

'Which one of you goons put this message under the stack

on my desk?' he inquired in a dangerously pleasant tone of voice. One hand went up. 'Never do that again,' snarled Mason. 'Messages are vital in this business. I need to know what is going on as fast as possible, not when I happen to find a bit of paper buried on my desk. Do you think I've got second sight?'

He snorted and went out for some fresh air. He thought he heard a muttered 'Yes' in reply to his question, but decided to ignore it. By and large they were not too bad a bunch.

Outside, the youngsters were coming back from school. The bus would soon bring back their seniors from Linxton. He walked across the square and looked bleakly up the main street. There were a few people about, going in and out of the shops. Was it always this quiet, or was it because of the death? Then he caught himself: which death? The death of the woman in the big house might well have more effect in a village like this than the violent death of a gamekeeper. Currents could run strange in a tight community, and Hughes definitely had not been popular. That was the one solid thing that came through from the reports. Here and there one percipient interviewer had noted not that there was unconcern at the death, but that there was a certain satisfaction at it. He must remember to have a word with that constable; it looked as though he might have a 'nose'.

He went back into the caravan. Crawford looked up.

'Right,' said Mason. 'I think we had better have a word with Mr Milne. Come in and I'll brief you, and then you can go and get him.'

Crawford looked at his watch. Mason caught the inference.

'I know. He'll be thinking about the end of work. There's no better time to catch someone than when he has other things on his mind.'

Crawford smiled—politely. An impartial observer might

have thought that he too had been thinking about the end of work for the day.

15

'So,' said Mason, some time later. 'You know absolutely nothing about the late Mr Hughes other than that he came here some five or six years ago.'

'That's right.'

Crawford shifted the weight from one foot to the other. Milne moved his head to keep him in view. Mason nodded to Crawford who took up the questioning.

'We were wondering whether you knew anyone who might have known Hughes better than that.'

Milne ignored him, and turned to glare at Mason. Mason had turned to look out of the window. Milne jerked his head back to Crawford, but said nothing.

'It's just that we have reason to believe that someone you know—one of your relatives, in fact—knew Hughes quite well,' explained Crawford mildly.

Milne shifted his legs to thrust his hands underneath him, then rocked forward. Mason turned at the movement. To him Milne looked as if he were before some high altar, and then, as Milne began to rock backwards and forwards, it seemed more as if he were at the Wailing Wall.

'You must have reason to ask,' said Milne at last.

'You seemed very angry at your sister's house this morning,' said Mason.

Milne continued to look at Crawford as he rocked, but replied, 'That was you this morning was it?'

'Yes.'

The rocking slowed.

'She had just told me,' said Milne. 'I was so ashamed.'

'That was the first you knew?' asked Crawford.

'Before God, that was the first.'

'Will you give us a statement to that effect?'

Milne nodded.

Crawford probed further. Where had Milne been on Friday? On Saturday? On Sunday?

Mason found himself thinking it all almost irrelevant. Somehow he knew this was getting them nowhere, though it would all have to be checked. And it sounded easily checked. The car electrical wholesalers north of Greyhavens would have records of the purchases on the Friday and doubtless would remember the man himself. Saturday, Milne had been on duty at the garage because the usual pump girl had been away at a wedding. And he had fixed the suspension of a client's car. Sunday was church—though in any event Drew-Drew had said the death had been on the Saturday.

Mason went out and sent in another constable. Crawford could take the statement; he himself needed to think. Clearly Milne had a flaring temper. Violent, even. What if he had heard of his sister's goings-on before this morning? Would he not have gone for the man? Mason's bruised face proved Milne could act without thinking. But would that temper have flared fiercely enough to have lasted the tramp from the road to where Hughes had been found, whichever way you walked in to the glen? Somehow he didn't think so, though it remained a possibility, just. But it would be easy enough probably to catalogue sufficient transactions at the garage to eliminate Milne simply on a matter of time. Presumably there would be credit-card transactions which they could use to find out who had bought petrol, and Milne himself might be able to give them a list as well.

Later Mason commended Crawford. 'If you had told him we knew that his sister knew Hughes intimately I would have had you off this case,' he grinned. 'These things can be nasty, and we would have lost a lot if he had riled up. You did well to avoid it. Always think ahead.'

Crawford allowed a small smile to play round his lips.

Mason followed the thought back to the encounter in the garage. He laughed out loud. 'That's right, lad. Learn by mistakes—preferably other people's. Well, I'm off home. I'll be back tomorrow.'

16

Despite her apparent air of self-possession, Mason could see that the woman was on edge. He had been careful to arrange the files on the top of his desk before she was due. The Hughes file was safely back at PenIron, but he took another fat file, wrote HUGHES in red across it, and had put it at one side of the desk with another file partly on top of it. He saw her side-long glance at the file as she sat down.

'Now, Mrs Bonaly. How can I help you?'

'I can help you,' came the reply in a low tone.

'Indeed?'

'It was a dreadful sight. Dreadful!'

Mason waited.

'That poor man. Struck down in the prime of his life. Gunned down by a false friend.'

Mason still waited.

'I can see him now. Lying there. Weltering in his blood. Clutching the heather in his vain attempt to get away.'

'I see,' said Mason. 'Were you there? Did you see what happened?'

'I saw. I saw. He was walking along, thinking of nothing when the shot struck. It came from a clump of trees. It was a woman.' The last words were hissed.

Mason leaned back in his seat and steepled his fingers. 'I am sorry, Mrs Bonaly,' he said. 'I think we are not talking about the same thing. Can you explain yourself further.'

'I have had a vision,' came the reply.

Mason gently, over the next few minutes, disengaged himself.

After he had sent Mrs Bonaly on her way with an assurance that he would consider what she had said, which was enough to pacify her, he went along to the Boss. He was not in. He left a note, and went back to his office. There was paper work for his other investigations to be dealt with, and there was no reason for him to go back to PenIron immediately. Crawford and Paget could keep things ticking over there. It was still a matter of getting in information and checking things. Once they had the basic facts clearer there would be a chance to put things together. In the words of one of the instructors at Police College, they were still at the stage of turning over the pieces so that all the picture sides of the jigsaw were face up. Yes, Cramond used to say, you could see that some were 'edgy bits', but until you got the coloured sides up you had a lot of problems with the rest.

Still, thought Mason, as he sat down and got the dictating machine out of his desk drawer, there were people like his old Great-aunt Daisy. In her time she had done so many jigsaws that she now enjoyed doing them plain side up. 'T'other way's too easy,' he had been told indignantly when, with the best of intentions, he had started to turn over the pieces of a new jigsaw for her.

He sighed, and pulled the pile of files towards him. With a grin he consigned the dummy Hughes file cover to the square filing cabinet at his side. Mrs Bonaly, indeed! Why hadn't he been warned? But there had been a woman in the vision. That did make some sort of sense. If it had been a sawn-off shotgun that would have been easily carried by a woman. And he knew of two women in the case. The Robertson female, he thought, could be excluded. But what of the other, the Joan who had sent the birthday card? Who was she? There were a number of Joan's on the Voters List for the district. Crawford had got one of the constables to check that, and of those, four at least had not yet been contacted. He stretched out his hand to the phone, but then changed his mind. Time enough to get going on that sort of detail at a later stage. Let's just get the pieces coloured side up for now.

He scanned the first file and started dictating.

17

It being Friday, Williams was in Greyhavens on hospital visiting. It was a fairly light afternoon for some reason, and he was grateful for that. He thought he would be able to get down into town later on. It was Paul's birthday in a couple of weeks, and he had promised Ann that when he could he would have a look round the shops to see what might be a surprise for their son. He was at that difficult age, when toys were just getting beneath his dignity.

In the long-term geriatric ward he settled beside Mrs Fletcher. She had been there for years, even back into Dr Jones's day, and Williams had wondered what he might find. Yet from the very first day they had got on well. He had gone into the ward looking for this parishioner of his who, he had been told, had no hope of ever getting back to PenIron unless in a coffin. She still had a small cottage waiting for her, for she had refused to sell it, but that was an impossibility. The impression he was given was that she was an intransigent old soul.

Instead he had found a clearly frail and helpless old body, with a lively pair of eyes and an acute interest in what was happening in 'her church'. It was true, she could only be cared for in a hospital, and yet she was in many important ways more lively than many on the parish roll. Increasingly he found himself looking forward to visiting her. From her he learned much wisdom, a deal of village history, and even a fair amount about the faith he had studied for those years in college.

'Sit ye down,' she said as soon as Williams appeared. 'What's this I'm hearing about the village?' The nurses had read to her the coverage of the murder in the *Greyhavens Gazette*, knowing she was always interested in any smidgeon of news of her village.

Williams told her briefly what had happened. As he did so the old lady closed her eyes.

When he finished she lay passive and silent, only a faint movement showing she was breathing. Williams waited, then, getting worried, moved his chair closer and leaned forward. At the sound of his chair scraping on the wooden floor she opened her eyes, looking straight upwards. Then she smiled.

'Ask Jessie,' she said. 'Ask Jessie to take you into my house and get the old photo albums in the cabinet in my bedroom. Bring them here.'

Williams was puzzled by the non-sequitur. Jessie Munro was the woman in the village who had charge of Mrs Fletcher's house. But what had this to do with what he had just told the old woman?

She smiled. 'Long winters,' she said. 'Long winters. But this winter has not been too bad, has it? I lose track in this place.' She glanced round, exasperated at the hospital cream walls.

Then she wanted to know how various people in the parish were doing, and conversation flowed for a few more minutes on births, an engagement and a retiral. But she tired easily. Williams had noticed this more and more in recent months. So he did not delay his departure.

18

Downtown he wandered through one or two toyshops, and saw nothing that really seemed 'right' for his son.

He was gazing into the window of another, which seemed depressing like the others, when a woman's voice interrupted his line of thought. He turned, welcoming the distraction. It was Betty Robertson. She seemed nervous.

'Could you come somewhere? I must talk to you,' she said.

In the nearby coffee-shop while he ordered he noticed that she was constantly looking around. Momentarily he wondered whether this was a case of 'crush-on-the-minister' and that she was hoping to be seen, but quickly realized that the opposite was true.

'What can I do for you?' he asked.

'Wait,' she said, and they waited in silence until the coffee arrived.

'I need help,' she began abruptly, bending over her cup as if to inspect the brew.

He stirred his coffee, and waited.

'I've been very foolish.'

'We're all foolish now and again.'

'Not like this.' She was exasperated. He bit his tongue. After a pause, she resumed.

'I need help,' she repeated, and went on steadily. 'I've lied to the police and I think they'll find out.'

She looked up at him, but he remained silent.

Colour flushed into her face as she resumed. 'Briefly, I had an affair with Evan Hughes.'

Williams felt as if a trowel had gone through his stomach. It was no good, he thought. Every time someone confessed to him something which he had thought them quite incapable of, he had that same sick feeling. No wonder ulcers were getting to be an occupational disease of the clergy.

But she did not notice anything amiss and went on.

'It's all over now—some time ago, actually. He threw me over.' She laughed wryly.

'And you've told the police you knew nothing about him?' Williams asked gently.

She shook her head.

'No. I told them about that. I had to. The Superintendent or whoever had found a letter of mine I had missed in Evan's cottage.'

She saw the question on Williams's face.

'I broke into his house when I heard he was dead. You see, I knew my letters were there and I had to get them back.'

Williams snorted briefly. This had an amusing element to it. One of his respectable, albeit younger, members confessing to breaking and entering. What next?

'So?' He prodded her with the monosyllable.

She looked puzzled.

'What's the problem? The break-in?'

'No. I had to tell him about that too. He saw my hand.' She showed the sticking plaster. 'When he came round it was still bandaged and had been bleeding.'

'Are they charging you with burglary?'

'No. At least I don't think so. Though I wouldn't put anything past that man. He is so . . . so . . .' She cast her mind back to Mason, sitting there in her room, playing cat-and-mouse with her. 'He's satanic, with the oddest eyebrow, as if he's been in a car crash, which doesn't help.'

Williams carefully filed away this opinion of his friend for future use.

'What, then?'

She picked up her spoon and toyed with it. It had a spot or something which she very carefully dealt with.

Williams waited.

At length she laid down the spoon and turned the depth of her eyes on to him.

'It's Keith,' she said. 'We both told the police that we were down in Perth that weekend. So we were. At least we went down there, but I don't know where Keith was on the Saturday night. He came back on the Sunday afternoon.'

'Oh.'

'So what do I do?'

'Does Keith know about you and Hughes?'

'I didn't think so. But now . . .' Her face showed signs of crumpling.

'Now you're worried that somehow he had found out, and killed Hughes by way of revenge. And you're worried that the police will find out that you've been concealing more things from them.'

She nodded.

Williams thought. Then he sighed.

'I think that honesty is always the best policy, particularly after some deceit. Do I assume from what you've said, or not said, that the Hughes thing was a passing matter and that your marriage is still salvageable?'

She gave a small nod, her face looking pinched as she did so. 'I hope so.'

'And can I assume that you don't really think that Keith did it.'

Another nod.

'Well, I think you would be best to make a clean breast of it—sorry, I didn't mean to put it like that. Tell Keith what has happened, and then go to the police, both of you, and explain the matter to them. They're not such ogres as all that, and, apart from giving you a scare to make sure you won't do it again, they'll probably be quite pleased to get you off their suspect list.'

She toyed with the spoon again.

'It's not as simple as that,' she said reluctantly. 'Where was Keith?'

It was his turn to nod.

'You want me to ask him?'

'Would you?'

'Anything else I should know?'

'I didn't stay in Perth either.'

'Where were you?'

'I said just now that I thought our marriage was salvage-able. I just don't know about that. Where was Keith? Was he away with someone else?'

'So you were away with someone else too?'

'No. No. I've learned my lesson about that. I went to Glasgow.' She laughed. 'I went to the opera.'

He lifted an eyebrow. 'Was it appropriate?'

'No.'

He did not pursue it.

'So there is a problem between you two, and that's why you're scared.'

'Yes. Can you help?'

'You will see him before I do.'

'Not if you would go round to his office this afternoon. That's what I thought as soon as I saw you outside that toy-shop,' she finished in a rush.

He was drained, when he got home. Ann saw the look in his face, and did not ask about the present for Paul. Or at least not until she had fed her husband.

19

Miss Anthony's funeral was on the Saturday.

There was a magic in the air, thought Williams, as he led the cortege out through the church door. Coming from the stone interior, hallowed though it was, into the freshness of the spring air made such a contrast. A few daffodils made a patch of colour against the duller green, and yet even that duller green had a tinge of the freshness to come.

Slowly he led the way across to the Anthony burial plot. There the tattered and muddy green tarpaulin laid over the pile of earth was intrusive and out of place. With a shock he realized that the earth was heaped over the grave of Harold Anthony, and immediately was grateful that there were no 'family' to take offence at that slight. James, the gravedigger, should have been more careful.

Williams walked slowly to the end of the grave and stood there while the undertaker's men placed the coffin on the battens. He then moved to the head of the coffin and himself took the head cord. He nodded to the others and they came forward. Peter Wade, Miss Anthony's man of business, took the cord at the foot. Old Isaac Watson, who had known Miss Anthony all his life, took a cord at the right, as did Douglas Milne of the garage. The cords on the left were taken by Colin Marsh and by Maxwell Hislop, the estate factor.

'Take the strain please, gentlemen,' came the undertaker's respectful tones.

The battens were removed. Williams began the committal service. As he came to the 'earth to earth' passage, the coffin was slowly lowered into the earth. With a detached part of his mind Williams watched it, down past the rich loam that was the foundation of the valley's prosperity, then past the pebble layer that he always noticed in this graveyard, and down into the clay beneath. The undertaker threw in a handful of soil, which sounded harsh in the quietness. From over the fields came the 'knee-naw' of a train. The two-thirty from Greyhavens, Williams said to himself.

He looked round the company. It was good to see how many had come to see the old lady to her last resting-place. What a contrast with the sparse attendance at the Hughes funeral. He glanced across to that grave on the opposite side of the graveyard, but could not see it from where he stood.

On impulse he began to speak.

'Friends, I thank you in the name of the Anthony family for coming. Yes, I know that there is now no Anthony family, but if we look around us we can see what that family has done in this pleasant valley for so many years and through so many generations.

'Miss Anthony was known by us all, and loved by most of us. Isaac here spoke to me the other night of playing in the Anthony orchard with Miss Anthony when she was a little girl, and others have similar memories of picnics at the big house, and kindnesses done. Let us give thanks to God for all that, and remember her with gratitude.

'Now, may the blessing of God our Father go with us all.' As he lifted his arms and blessed his flock, again a pang went through him. This was such a contrast with the Hughes funeral.

'Now, if anyone would like to come into the church hall, there is a cup of tea.'

The gathering was slow to disperse. When Williams came out of the vestry there were still groups seated at the tables talking in lowered tones. He went over to where Ann was with Mrs Jenkins and some of the women.

'That was a lovely service,' said Mrs Jenkins as he came up. 'So inspiring.'

'Thank you,' said Miss Andrews. Mrs Marsh and Mrs Maddon smiled.

Williams drew Ann aside. 'It might be good if we were to invite old Isaac and one or two of the other folk to the manse. They've got a lot of memory to cover, and it would be more comfortable down there.'

Ann made a not-too-pleased face at him, and clearly meant it, but then brightened.

'I suppose you're right,' she said. 'Pity you hadn't thought of that earlier.'

*

Williams was quite right. The older people did appreciate a chance to sit comfortably in the manse lounge and swap stories.

'You got it right, Minister,' said Isaac Watson expansively. 'They was a family, a good family. Not but what they weren't all saints, but they was a good family. Not stuck up. Caring.'

'You're right there,' said old Alfred Milne, sitting beside his son and attending to his pipe. 'I remember once Miss Anthony coming to the house when we had the diphtheria. Or was it the polly-molly-lightis.'

'Don't look at me, Dad,' said Douglas Milne. 'That was before my time.'

'So it was, so it was. I suppose it was before we had started into cars and tractors. Old Julius was still shoeing horses round the back there.'

'Julius?' ventured Williams, and the old man cackled.

'Julius. Julius. That was his name. He came over from the Continent before the First World War and got a job with my father shoeing horses. He was from Austria or Bavaria or some -aria. They thought of locking him up in that War being an enemy, but old Donald Anthony, Miss Anthony's father, he spoke up for him.'

'Donald. Wasn't that the name of Harold Anthony's father?' asked Williams.

Isaac Watson took up the thread. 'Indeed so. It was that.'

Williams felt that the time was propitious for the answer to a question.

'It has always puzzled me why Miss Anthony's brother went to Australia and stayed there.'

Watson coughed, and looked into the fire. Alfred Milne got out his matches and struggled to relight his pipe. The silence grew strained.

'Well,' said Williams at last, 'tell me, you who know this valley, was this last winter as bad as it seemed?'

'There's been worse,' said Isaac Watson, rising to his feet.

'Yes. We had better be going,' added Alfred Milne. 'It was right civil of you to ask us old 'uns back to the manse. That is something new, and I approve.'

Ann went for the coats, and Williams helped Milne on with his.

Milne turned and tapped Williams on the chest with his pipe.

'You know, laddie,' he said, 'you said a lot of right things about Miss Mildred, not least that she was loved by most of us. Not all of us. She could have a tongue in her head that would cut you to the bone, and some would never forgive that, for she was always right. That's why her brother went to Australia.'

Isaac Watson came across, listening. Then he chipped in. 'Work your dates out,' he said. 'That'll tell you why he left.'

'So what did Isaac Watson mean?' asked Ann later that evening.

'I don't know,' replied Williams. 'I don't know what dates he was talking about, and I don't know what any dates would mean in any case.'

'Well, what dates do we know about?'

'All I know is that Mildred Anthony was eighty-six.'

'So how old was her brother?'

'I don't know. She told me once that he was a few years younger than she was, but he went out to Australia pretty soon after the War.'

'Which war?'

'The Second, I suppose.'

'But why all the mystery? When you asked that question it was as if a bomb had gone off. Not a loud bomb, a silence bomb. It all went so quiet.'

'You know, sometimes I think I am getting to know this place, that I'm coming to be one of the community. Then something like that happens. Something's said or done which proves that I am still an outsider, an incomer, not part of things at all.'

Ann came and sat beside him and put an arm round his hunched shoulders.

'Time, dear. Time. In another forty years you too will be on the inside looking out.'

'That's just it. We should never have folk out looking in.'

'You're wrong there.' She gave him an affectionate shake. 'Until you are part you cannot but be apart.'

'Even among the church?'

'Even among the church, and even in heaven. Remember Jesus had three favourites, and of those one was the favourite above all.'

'Where's your theology degree from?'

She smiled. 'The Bible. Didn't they use that at your college?'

'Not really. It was just a strop for them to sharpen their wits on.'

She laughed.

'You know,' he went on. 'I wonder at the rubbish those academics talk. They escape into Divinity and never come out.'

'That's not fair.'

'It's more true than not.'

'So?'

'So why do we have these half-men involved in training —training!—folk for the ministry?'

'That's a long way from the question.'

'What question?'

'Why did Harold Anthony go to Australia?'

'I don't know. In any event it wasn't Harold. Harold was the one that came back. Donald was the one that went away.'

Ann jumped to her feet. 'That's it,' she said, and paced round the room.

Williams looked his question.

'No, it isn't,' she said, and sat down again.

The phone went. Briefly Williams thought of allowing the answering machine to do its duty, but then he shrugged and went into the study.

Ann watched the fire, wistfully. Her mind skittered back to her childhood. Her father had told her wondrous stories of salamanders, and she had sat for hours as a child, looking and looking, hoping that one day a salamander would put its snout out through the grate and speak to her.

He came back, his face serious.

'I'm afraid Mrs Fletcher has had a stroke,' he said. 'That was Jessie Munro. They phoned her. Pity. Mrs F. asked me to bring in some photo book or other on Thursday. It would have been interesting to hear her go over some of the old scenes.'

20

The following Thursday evening found Mason in London. The Hughes investigation had apparently run into the sand. The incident caravan had been staged down, though there was little enough to go on, but the sifting of the various interviews would take some little time. Nothing had jumped off the pages on a quick scrutiny, and there was no sense in doing in the caravan what could be more comfortably done in headquarters.

It was as he had looked again at the solicitor's letter he had taken from the floor of Hughes's living-room that a ploy had occurred to Mason. And the Real Boss had given him the chance—the immediate Boss was on holiday. With a twinkle in his eye, the Real Boss had been willing both to let him go down to London, and stay overnight so as to see Eric in the evening.

Sitting with his son in the Royal Festival Hall waiting for the second half of the concert to begin, Mason allowed himself to reflect on the day. He had come down on the early plane, done his visits to the Bank and to the lawyers, had something to eat, and had met Eric outside the Festival Hall bookshop.

In fact he had cheated. The arrangement had been to meet outside the shop, but Mason had gone into the bookshop. He told himself that he wanted to look through the miniature scores—since he had been a boy he had liked occasionally to listen to music with a score in front of him, though his collection of scores was very thin. Maybe he would manage to pick up something on one of his favourite pieces, he had told himself. But really he had gone in so that he would be sure of seeing his son before he was seen.

It had worked. Eric came briskly up the stairs and stood looking around. He looked well. Obviously he was fit, interested in life, on top of his job. The world's his oyster, thought Mason, and then wondered if his son had ever yet eaten that dainty. Still, he was proud of him. No wonder his mother had been pleased to see him looking so well, though she had detected signs of homesickness. Mason saw nothing of that. Maybe it was just wishful thinking on Jane's part. Or maybe that it was that she had had longer to spend with their son. Mason wished he could prolong things too. But, he sighed, duty called.

Eric caught the sigh, and looked quickly at his Dad, but, apart from a slight smile, there was nothing to be seen.

During the first half of the programme Mason had firmly repressed any tendency to let his mind wander back to the Hughes business. But the prospect of Stravinsky's 'Rite of Spring' led him to think of it again. The elemental nature of that music fitted both life and violent death, he mused. It fitted also what he had been told.

Once he had identified himself to the bank manager, the man had been quite cooperative. Really very cooperative, for there was little that he could tell Mason. The deceased had had two accounts at the branch, but did little operating on them other than to draw cheques at regular intervals. The payments in came in the form of monthly cheques from a firm of lawyers in the City. The manager let Mason see the file in which the regular letters acknowledging receipt of the cheques were kept. It was the same firm with which Mason had an appointment that afternoon.

'Why don't they use credit transfer?' Mason had wanted to know, but the manager had merely shrugged. It was not for him to question instructions.

The lawyer had been less cooperative. Unlike the banker, he had carefully checked Mason's identity card, and then had settled into his expensive-looking chair. Mason found himself disliking him. He was what Mason termed a shell of a man—efficient, yet curiously empty. He seemed smug, quite unconcerned about the violent death. Yes, he knew the source of the funds that were paid into the Hughes account. Yes, Hughes had himself been in touch quite recently with a question. But, no, he did not feel himself at liberty without the instructions of his client to inform Mason about these matters. Yes, he would get instructions, but that might take some time. Yes, he would send on the information if permission was forthcoming.

Mason had hoped for more, but had to take what he could get. He absorbed the extra hour or so in the afternoon poking about in the second-hand bookshops in Charing Cross Road looking for railway books.

The Stravinsky began. It was the first time that Mason had heard it in the flesh. It was magnificent. From his vantage-point high in the mezzanine seats Mason could see the whole orchestra, and follow physically the strenuous bowing as it rippled through the divisions of the orchestra. And behind all, particularly towards the end, the white heads of the drumsticks pounded out their cross-rhythms.

Eric said little when it was finished. But clearly, he was impressed.

21

One week later a letter arrived from the firm of London solicitors. As he read it Mason's eyebrows twitched.

Dear Superintendent,

I was very concerned to learn from you of the circumstances of the passing of Evan Hughes. Accordingly I took the liberty of phoning, rather than writing our instructing clients, a firm of solicitors in South Australia. They have spoken to the Trustees involved, and I am authorized to inform you of the following facts.

As you surmised, Hughes was in touch with us regarding the source of the funds that were transmitted to him—a regrettable lapse by his Bank gave him our name. Indeed, he had written several letters since late autumn last year, letters of a pressing nature. We were, however, under instructions not to inform him of any details.

Evan Hughes was the beneficiary of a trust set up by the late Donald Anthony, of whom he was the illegitimate son. That Trust terminates on Hughes's death and the capital is destined otherwise. Donald Anthony set up the Trust in 1946, when it was dealt with by ourselves. However, he transferred it to Australia when he emigrated there in 1950.** He died, at the age of 79 in 1984.

I believe that Hughes was reared on the estate of a family friend of Donald Anthony (a not unknown phenomenon) (though one of my senior colleagues believes that that estate once formed part of the Anthony holdings) and the financial provision for his upkeep made through us was as I have stated. Until he reached the age of majority the payments were made to his 'foster' parents, but thereafter were made to him through the agency of the Bank.

So far as we are aware no one knew of this connection, and I was surprised to learn from you that he was employed on the estate of the person who must have been his natural aunt. We have no explanation for this.

Whether this information will assist you in clarifying the circumstances of his death, I cannot say. Whether there is anything else that we can help with, I also cannot say. But rest assured that I have been given full authority to assist you in any way that I can.

Yours faithfully,
B. Candlish

** (Technically he terminated the former Trust and set up a new one.) B.C.

Mason massaged the back of his neck as he mulled over the contents of the letter. Did it complicate or ease the picture? Did it provide a motive for the death? Who would benefit from the death? No one that he could think of. Hughes being illegitimate would not have inherited from anyone, would he?

His mouth twisted with a slight grin as he thought of what would have happened if Hughes had inherited from his 'aunt'. That would have set the cat among the pigeons down in PenIron, to have their local rogue installed in the 'big house'. That would have been a sight indeed. But—he sobered—it was not going to happen and instead he was trying to solve the violent death of the . . . the . . .?

Something was pricking at the back of his mind.

He went over to the bookcase behind his desk and pulled out a basic Law text. A few minutes searching brought him the answer that illegitimate children had been given some rights of succession, but only from their parents, back in 1968. So that didn't apply.

Absently he wondered who Miss Anthony had left her

estate to. Not that it looked as though it was a good inheritance. It had had a seedy air about it, and that man—what was his name? the one who had given him the key to Hughes's cottage—he didn't look as though he cared much about the estate. It was just a comfortable source of pay for limited needs, not a good going business. Presumably there was a cash-flow problem somewhere and the estate had not been managed as well as it required to retain its vitality. Still, that was not his concern.

Nor was the Hughes business his single problem. There were other things to be seen to as well. Crime doesn't wait to let the police solve each offence in turn.

He pulled out the Hughes file, dictated a brief note of thanks to the London solicitor, added the London letter to the file and put it in his Pending tray to await the carbon of his response. Then he turned to other matters.

FIVE: MAY

1

April turned to May. Williams got going with his motor-mower trimming the great swathe of lawn that lay in front of the manse, though leaving the patches where the daffodils had been so that next year's bulbs would be well-nourished and fit once more to bedeck their garden with that glorious yellow which is the hall-mark of the King Alfred. Round the back, he set to work putting in vegetables now that the earth was warming. In previous years he had tried seeds, but now, on the advice of old Isaac Watson, was putting in plants bought from a garden centre on the outskirts of Greyhavens.

'For all you're needing,' the old man had said, 'you might as well put in plants. Put in seeds and you're feeding the birds.'

Towards the end of the month Mason came to visit. The incident caravan had been withdrawn at the end of the first week in May, and Williams had neither seen nor heard from his friend since. He had gathered that there was still some police activity in the village on the Hughes business, but noticed in the *Gazette* that Mason was also now involved in another investigation to the north of Greyhavens.

'It's no good,' said Mason heavily as he sat and watched Williams work on the railway. 'I am afraid we can't pin the Hughes business on anyone. There's no one who fits the bill. Plenty of motive for several males. All the women seem to have a much more relaxed attitude—no avenging angels among them. None of them seem to have turned into harpies when they were tossed aside. But out of it all there is nothing.'

Williams looked up from where he was adjusting a de-railed goods train. Then he came across, pulled out a stool and sat down beside Mason who was at the control console.

'I'm not sure if I'm glad to hear that, or very sorry,' he said.

'Mixed feelings? How?' Mason lifted his crooked eyebrow.

'Well, on the one hand, as you indicate, Hughes was a disruptive element. It will take years for some of the wounds he inflicted that I know of to heal, and I deduce from the way you put it, that there was more going on.'

Mason nodded. 'I'm sorry, but there was quite a lot going on—and may still be some. Hughes wasn't the only local offender.'

'I don't think I want to know any more than that,' replied Williams. 'It is a worrying thing to hear you say, though.'

'But there may be some good out of it. Just reading the statements, and talking to some of the people involved makes me sure that some of them have taken thought to themselves.'

'That's true. One of the marriages I know of I would almost say has bounced back quite remarkably. And there is the matter of Maddon's daughter.'

'When is the child due? I can't remember, if we ever knew.'

'In about three months.'

'How are things?'

'They were very difficult for a while. But I gather that Peter Wade has managed things quite well.'

'Oh?'

'Yes. Apparently because the court action had been raised, and there is documentary evidence that Hughes had accepted that he was the father, the child will inherit his estate, and there was quite a bit of it once things were sorted out.'

'He had accepted it? How?'

'I remember Peter Wade told me before the death that Hughes had written him accepting responsibility, but even so the Maddons, or rather the girl, had had to sue him. I seem to remember that if there is a court judgment, the father can get income tax relief.'

'Surely that's not true any more. Once children's allowance was taken off Income Tax and was put on to a system of social security payment to the mothers, the question of the court decree would have been irrelevant.'

'You know a lot about it.'

'Well, I suppose I could be wrong. But in my line of business you get to know a bit about that sort of thing. Too many of the youngsters you pull in have a broken home background. In any event there may be special rules where there is no marriage involved. Or it could be that there just was a dispute about the amount of maintenance that was to be paid.'

'Well, anyway. It seems that there was that letter by Hughes. The point is that that gives the child a claim on his estate.'

'I looked that up too. But does it apply if the father has died before the birth?'

'Apparently, if it is clear who the father was. In this case there is his letter.'

'It's funny, you know. I had thought that the position about illegitimate children inheriting from parents was recent, but it's been the case in Scotland since 1968. Curious to think the change was so long ago. I bet most folk don't realize it.'

'Yes. They tell me there was another widening recently, that illegitimate children have the same rights as legitimate ones in the estate of their parents, according to Peter Wade. Then it's just a matter of whether the parenthood can be proved. In this case the Crown is satisfied by that letter to Wade from Hughes.'

'The Crown? Oh yes, of course. Hughes had no relatives. His property would have fallen to the Crown.'

'Yes. There's some grand-sounding person in Edinburgh who deals with these matters.'

'The Queen's and Lord Treasurer's Remembrancer, if memory serves.'

'Yes. That's right. So there do remain some traces of your time at law school.'

'Shards and shreds, as the Boss said the other day.'

'So the Crown is not going to claim the estate.'

'That's what Peter Wade has said. So long as some other relative of Hughes doesn't pop out of the woodwork, that is. It would be just the thing if he had a child down in Wales. But that's being looked into.'

'Well, for what it's worth there was nothing in his bank transactions that would indicate any regular payments of that kind.'

Williams raised his eyebrows at the comment, and resumed. 'The result is that whatever remains of the Hughes estate, and I gather there was quite a bit in his bank, will go to the child. The mother will, of course, look after that, but she will be advised by Peter Wade. He's handling that side of things for the Maddons.'

Mason yawned. He was feeling very tired. 'So it's all happened for the best?'

'Yes.' Williams grinned. 'But don't worry. The Crown isn't getting nothing from PenIron. It seems Miss Anthony had left the bulk of her estate, including the property, to Harold Anthony, and hadn't got around to changing that after his death. So that falls into intestacy, and, since there is no heir, it goes to the Crown. Pity. It may mean the break-up of the property and will mean a hole at the heart of the community.'

'Nothing to the church?'

'She did make several other bequests, including £5000 to the church. That'll help us with the roof problems we've got.'

'So—mixed feelings.'

'Mixed feelings. That's right. You were asking why I had mixed feelings about Hughes. The point is that that particular canker in the community has been removed. But, of course, on the other hand there remains the awful feeling that there may be a murderer loose somewhere in the village. That's not good for the community either.'

'Noticed anything?'

Williams glanced shrewdly at his friend, then shook his head.

'No. There's no one I've noticed going around with the mark of Cain on his forehead.'

Mason leaned over and punched him on the upper arm.

'Come on, Ted,' he said. 'You of anyone I know shouldn't make that mistake.'

'Mistake?' Williams was puzzled.

Mason turned to the console and started the trains running.

'Allow me to instruct you,' he said. 'If you were to look at Genesis, you would find that the mark of Cain was put on him to protect him, not to identify him to the local police.'

Williams laughed, and the two gave themselves up to timetable-keeping, and moved a large quantity of goods from the sidings at Milliburgh round to the sea-port at Johnshaven.

At length Williams asked a question.

'So what happens now with the Hughes business?'

'The file remains open, but unless something turns up, I reckon it will become one of those unsolved cases.'

'Your first?'

'First unsolved murder. Though—' he looked at Williams —'there was one in which I was considerably helped by an amateur.'

Williams laughed. 'Not me. I'm not going to turn into your spy in the community.'

Ann came in with coffee and newly baked bran muffins with butter on their tops, melting into them. She laid the tray down on an area of the staging which Mason quickly cleared. Williams fetched another stool from the back of the room.

'Alan's trying to recruit me,' Williams told her.

'I hope you informed him we're quite happy here,' she replied.

'No, no. Not into the police, though sometimes a change of profession does seem a good idea.'

It was Mason's turn to laugh. 'You'd never pass the physical,' he said.

'I don't know about that. I've taken up jogging,' said Williams mock-aggrievedly. He turned to Ann. 'No. He wants me to be a stool-pigeon.'

'How appropriate,' said Ann, negligently swinging her foot against the stool Williams was sitting on, and all three shared the humour.

'I wasn't really,' said Mason.

'But if I happened to notice anything, you would expect me to get in touch.'

Mason raised his broken eyebrow, and for a moment Ann thought he looked quite satanic the way that the spotlights above the railway track shadowed his face.

'All I asked was whether you had noticed anything these weeks.' To Ann: 'I was saying that we had run ourselves into the sand. There are plenty of motives, but in each case we've eliminated the person.'

'Someone eliminated Hughes,' Ann observed darkly, and shivered.

'Yes. We always come back to that.'

'There's no doubt it was murder?'

'None. We have searched the area where the body was found and there is, or rather was, no gun.'

'You are sure that he was killed there?'

'Yes.'

'But how can you be?' asked Ann with a fierceness that surprised Mason.

Mason put down his mug. 'You really want to know?'

'No.' Then after a pause Ann said, 'Yes. Yes, I do want to know. You've been talking about the thing to Ted, and I've gathered some things through him, but I'd prefer to hear it direct from you. It's an awful feeling to go down the street and see people, and find yourself thinking, "Was it you?" or "Was it you?"'

'Maybe I should have asked you rather than Ted whether you've noticed anything,' said Mason drily. 'No, there is no doubt that Hughes was shot where he was found. The Forensic Medicine folk are clear about that.'

Mason stopped and looked at Williams. Williams nodded, so Mason continued, his eyes on his mug.

'He was shot at close range with a sawn-off shotgun. The shot had balled a bit so it was more destructive. The blast tore into his lower chest and abdomen, and threw him back on to the ground exactly where he was found. The marks on the jacket he had on are consistent with that. He had fallen backward. Clearly fallen. There was no evidence that the body had been dragged. Further, as the shot had balled there was a fair leakage of blood. The soaking hadn't been altered or changed the way it would have been if the body had been moved after the shot. The ghouls—sorry—the Forensic people say that the wound was such as to cause a massive loss of blood pressure almost immediately, but it would have drained if the body had been moved any distance. As it was, the bulk of the drainage that had happened was on-site.'

Mason stopped, and glanced up at his audience. Ann was looking blankly at him.

'I'm sorry,' he said quietly. 'But you did ask.'

She shook her head briefly, as if to rid her vision of something. 'I see,' she said slowly. 'Poor you. It must be awful to have to deal with things like that.' Then she clearly pulled herself together, turned and picked up the plate.

'Have another muffin?'

'Thanks,' said Mason, taking one. Then he sat and looked at it. The butter was half melted, draining into the brown texture beneath it. He put it down on his plate.

Ann, busy with her own thoughts, didn't notice. Williams did.

'I see,' said Ann. 'Yes. Of course. I'm sure we would tell you anything we saw that looked odd to us, but I've not seen anything out of the ordinary in anyone. Have you?' She turned to her husband.

'No. That's what I was saying when you came in.'

'I thought you were saying you wouldn't be a stool-pigeon,' returned Mason.

'I was saying that I would not be a spy. But if there were anything I noticed or found out, of course I would get in touch. That would be a matter of public duty. The only problem would be if the murderer or murderess came and confessed to me.'

'Perhaps it's just as well that you don't have a confessional,' said Mason.

'You'd be surprised what has been said downstairs in the study.'

'But getting back to the matter,' said Ann. 'I've seen nothing odd about any one since it happened. I'd even say there has been an improvement. Betty and Keith, for instance.'

Mason smiled.

'Of course,' Ann went on, 'you found one of her letters. She was mortified, you know. But she also said to me that perhaps it was for the best. It made her make a clean breast of things to Keith.'

'It was mutual, apparently,' Williams put in, 'when you checked him out and found out where he had been. He had told her he was away checking stock, but she had other suspicions.'

'I don't know about this,' said Ann, curious.

Mason spread his hands. 'Well, there was nothing sinister about it. It was just that when my officers interviewed them they said that they were at the Perth horse sales. But when we checked things out he had not been there. She was definite. She said they were together all the time. Instead we found he had been away overnight.'

'You mean it could be Keith?' said Ann. 'But you've not arrested him?'

'Now you're jumping to conclusions. You're right. For a while it put him on my list as being unaccounted for.'

'But . . .' began Williams.

'I know. She came back to us after talking to you,' said Mason. 'But that wasn't enough. We had to exclude him by independent evidence. He could have driven up and walked in over the hill, shot Hughes and gone back down to Perth.'

'But Keith couldn't have walked that far,' said Ann slowly. 'He's got a steel leg from an accident when he was in the Air Force. I'm sure he couldn't have gone that distance.'

'Has he now?' said Mason. 'Neither of them mentioned that, though I suppose I do remember he walks with a limp. No matter. The point was that he was absent. She didn't know where he was. In fact he had gone off on a drinking bout with some old pals from his past. Apparently he used to do that quite regularly. She thought he was off with a woman, and I think that was one of the reasons why she was susceptible to Hughes.'

'So she was protecting him, even though she thought there was a chance he had found out about Hughes and had shot him,' said Ann. She clapped her hands. 'That's a better story than the one she told me. She said she had confessed and he had forgiven her.'

'Yes. It went a good deal deeper than that,' said Williams. He leaned back. 'Robertson had the beginnings of a drinking problem. He had managed to keep it out of her sight pretty well. But the effect was that they were drifting apart. She thought he was cooling, and certainly he was away on undisclosed "business" with those friends now and again. She thought there was another woman. It does also explain her and Hughes, you know.'

'Some friends,' said Ann.

Williams smiled. 'But by the time Betty told Alan about Hughes, he had had to tell Alan where he had in fact been. So he told her too. That was your idea, wasn't it?' he said to Mason.

Mason shrugged.

'You're a dear,' said Ann, getting up and giving him a hug. 'So that's the full story. I thought Betty was keeping something back. I suppose no woman wants to tell another woman she has had suspicions about what her husband is up to.'

'Well,' she went on, collecting the mugs and plates, 'I'd better get these things away.'

'Which is a polite way of saying I should be going,' observed Mason, looking at his watch.

She stuck out her tongue at him.

'In any event,' said Mason drawing himself to his full height preparatory to leaving, 'if anything does strike you . . .'

'Yes, sir,' chorused the other two.

2

Mason was restless that night. Something was escaping him. He had had that feeling before. His subconscious knew that there was some particle of information somewhere between his ears that was important. On the other hand he also

knew that the way to let it pop out into his conscious thinking
was to go to sleep, or to get on with other things.

About three a.m. it came to him.

He put on the bedside light and jotted down on the pad
that he kept for such emergencies.

'Hughes—illegitimate—Maddon   child . . .??   Inheritance.'

But in the morning it did not mean too much to him until
he was parking his car.

He phoned Williams as soon as he could, and was less
than pleased to hear his friend's voice inform him that he
was busy and would be checking his answering machine at
11.30. But the return call did come in on time.

'You remember you said something last night about recent changes in the law relating to illegitimate children?'
asked Mason.

'Yes.'

'What did you mean?'

'Well, I didn't know much about it, but I was driving
home the other night from Presbytery with Ian Paterson of
PenIron. We had had another turgid report from the Social
Committee, and we were speaking about the way the Law
has been changing. We're getting away from a proper moral
basis to Law and getting over on to expediency.'

'So?' Mason was impatient.

'I was telling Ian something Peter Wade's assistant had
said to me back in March, when Peter had his accident. She
said that the Law on illegitimate children had moved quite
away from a Christian marriage basis.'

'And?'

'Ian said that was right. Like you said, illegitimate children have had some right of inheritance from their parents
for a couple of decades but that that has now been extended
to include other relationships.'

'Has it now?'

Williams waited.

'Well,' said Mason, 'we would need to check things out as to the Law—I'll do that here—but, if it's true, there is a chance that your Iris Maddon's child will inherit the PenIron Estate, the Grey House and all.'

'What?'

'It seems that Hughes was the illegitimate son of Donald Anthony, which makes him Miss Anthony's nephew. If there is no other claimant, then presumably the child will get it through her father.'

Mason could hear the silence at the other end of the phone. Then Williams started to laugh.

'Well, that will be a turn-up for the books. Are you sure?'

'I'm sure as to the relationship between Miss Anthony and Hughes. I've got a solicitor's letter about that. And you said last night that the relationship between Hughes and the child was also established.'

Williams started to laugh. 'It does make sense. Now you mention it, there were similarities . . . If you let me know when you are sure about the legal end of it, I'll tell Peter Wade.'

'Wade?'

'He's acting for the Maddons.'

'Oh yes. So he is.'

That call over, Mason put in a call to Johnstone, whom he knew taught Law at Greyhavens University. That was irregular, but they were friends.

An hour later Johnstone returned the call. The law was as Williams had understood it. The change had been made for Scotland with effect from the beginning of the year, and a similar provision was being enacted in England. That would take effect next year. Where was the domicile of the persons concerned?

'The property's in Scotland.'

'And the people?'

'Scottish, I think. One of them was born in England, but has worked in Scotland for years. Fifteen years at least.'

'With property here?'

'A rented house.'

'Anything down south?'

'No.'

'In that case he or she would probably be domiciled here.'

'And?'

'And therefore there would be no problem. In any event if the child is born in Scotland, the Scots courts can deal with it. If the property's here then our rules apply.'

'Thanks.'

Williams had had time to think before Mason phoned. He was still pleased to know what the result of Mason's inquiries had been, and said he would get in touch with Wade that evening. There were some matters of church business to be dealt with, and he would raise this Hughes development then. Still, he had some reservation about how the village would take the news. But it would be better that someone like the Maddons take over the estate than have it sold, as was likely when it seemed there was no heir.

'Maddon's an accountant, isn't he?'

'Didn't you interview him?'

'No. But he was interviewed.'

'Yes, he is.'

'Any good at business?'

'I believe so.'

'Good,' concluded Mason. 'That estate needs someone to put a bomb under it.'

'I agree,' said Williams. 'It could be the main nerve of this village, but things have slid since Miss Anthony was not too well, and there wasn't the money to do things.'

'Quite. Well, maybe things will change now.'

3

That evening Williams sat on the sofa in front of the fire in Wade's large drawing-room. Wade had gone out to get some letter or other which he said clarified the point about the method of calculating how much each congregation had to remit to central church funds.

As so often before, he let his eyes travel round the elderly furnishings. Briefly he again wondered at the comments which some, like Mrs Jenkins, had made about the money which lay behind Bridge House. There didn't seem to be much sign of that, apart from the expensive car in the drive outside. It was curious how Wade appeared not to have altered anything that his father and mother had installed. Indeed, there was a Victorian feel to this room. This room—it came to Williams—he had only ever been in this room, and the hall. Perhaps the other rooms held more.

He got up and went over to the fireplace to look more carefully at the picture above the mantelpiece. Close up, the pastoral scene lost its appeal when seen from a distance. The brushwork was remarkably coarse when you examined it. Williams had thought that the Victorian pastoralists had been a bit better in their technique than that.

When Wade came back in, Williams was again on the sofa.

'There,' said Wade, holding out a duplicated letter, 'that contains the analysis of how the eventual figures are arrived at. It seems to me as though we have a good case that the Committee's figures do not take enough account of our extraordinary expenditures on the guttering and that sort of thing. It is open to them to make such allowances.'

The two men discussed business for a little longer, and

then Williams felt that it was time to introduce the new subject.

'I had Superintendent Mason on the phone. He gave me some information which I thought I should draw to your attention in connection with Iris Maddon's baby.'

'Yes? What might that be?'

'It seems that Evan Hughes was the illegitimate son of Donald Anthony.'

Wade sat back and put his hands flat on the arms of his chair. There was a brief silence, then he asked, 'He's sure about this?'

'Yes.'

Wade sat forward. 'That is very interesting. Very interesting. How did he find out?'

'I believe that the information came up through his investigations into Hughes's past.'

Wade nodded.

'If you think about it,' went on Williams, 'Hughes did look like Miss Anthony. Once I was told of the connection, I could see the resemblance.'

Wade pursed his lips. 'You mean there is a chance she was his mother?'

'No, no.' Williams waved the suggestion away. 'That's not possible.'

'You realize what this means?' Wade asked.

'Not really. But I wondered whether it meant that there would be any claim to the PenIron estate, seeing you told me there is the claim to anything Hughes left.'

Wade smiled broadly. 'It actually means that the child will inherit the PenIron estate. It wouldn't have done so until this year, but the law changed at the beginning of the year. Well, well, well.' He got up and, rubbing his hands together, went and stood in front of the fire.

'I'll need to check into this, of course.'

'I could give you the name of the London solicitor,' said Williams. 'Confidentially, of course. I just happen to know.'

Wade cracked a smile at that. 'I see,' he said. 'Well, you
do that and I'll get on to the matter at once. It will be better
for us all, of course. If PenIron went to the Crown, it would
just be sold and perhaps split up. Not that it is too great a
catch as it is. It does need proper management, but it could
be made to work out.'

He saw the slight puzzlement on Williams's face, and
went on, 'I know what you're thinking. Everyone knows I
have had—had—' he corrected himself—'power of attorney
for Miss Anthony for a good number of years, but it was
not an independent power. I had to consult regularly. I was
restricted in what I could do, and she was against change
and modernization. If I had been too bold, she would have
recalled the power and that would have been that.'

Williams nodded. 'I see.'

'Does it make any difference with the estate of Harold
Anthony?' he asked.

'I don't think so,' said Wade. 'But I'd need to find that
out too. Let me see now. He and Hughes would have
been half-brothers in blood.' He looked up at the ceiling,
frowning, and then his face cleared.

'Well, there would be no claim under our law, for that
changed only at the turn of the year. But I'll need to find
out what the position was under whatever Australian state
law applied to Anthony's estate. Still, I did write some
letters for Miss Anthony thereafter. I'm sure that there was
a will in that case, which took the property somewhere else
entirely. I'll check it out.'

'Good,' said Williams, rising to his feet. He held out his
hand. 'I'm glad Iris has you looking after her affairs, and
that there may be such a satisfactory outcome to all this. It
is some little gleam of light in it all.'

Wade nodded.

As he shrugged his way into his coat, Williams added,
'You know, I'm really rather down about all this.' He felt
about in his pockets for his gloves, and looked up into

Wade's eyes. 'You'll feel it worse than me, I suppose, being local. But to have the possibility that someone in the village . . .' He waved a glove dismissively. 'It doesn't bear thinking about.'

Wade nodded solemnly as he showed him out.

SIX: JUNE

1

It was Ann who brought the news of the newcomer.

'I hear that some newspaper reporter has bought the Maxwells' house,' she said idly at breakfast after the children had been sent on their way.

'Well,' said Williams, 'that's good. They will be pleased. It has been—what? three months since they moved south?'

'Three and a half.'

'It's not nice having two houses on your hands. Bank interest on bridging loans and the like.'

'That's true. I've heard of a few folk in Greyhavens who have been caught that way and have had eventually to put both houses on the market, and ended up selling the one they had just bought.'

'Well, it's not a worry we'll have.'

'Until we're old and grey and too doddery to bother about it.'

'True. I've been meaning actually to have a word with Peter Wade to see whether we oughtn't to buy somewhere and rent it out so that we will have somewhere to go to eventually.'

Ann contemplated far into the future and shivered.

'Maybe the Lord will come first,' she said.

'And in the meantime, do you know who has rescued the Maxwells?'

'No, I don't. It was Miss Andrews who was speaking. I met her in the butcher's yesterday.'

'Oh well, if she doesn't know, then no one does.'

'Ted!'

'It's true. She and Mrs Jenkins are the gossip-mill of PenIron.'

'I know. But it doesn't help to say it. And it does keep them going. I don't know what either of them would do without gossip to keep them interested.'

'I remember when I first met Mrs Jenkins, she was formidable in that upper-crust way she goes on. But she made it quite clear that I was on probation and that she knew a lot more about me than any incoming minister could expect. She had been on to some of her pals from Langbank, I gather from something which Miss Andrews let slip later. So she knew all about us.'

'No!'

'Yes. So, as I say, if she doesn't know who is coming, then no one does.'

But whether Williams was wrong or right, by the time he himself met Mrs Jenkins that morning as she was out shopping, the gossip-exchange had come through with the goods.

'I hear that the senior reporter from the *Greyhavens Gazette* is to come among us,' she observed. 'A newspaperman.' Her inflection made her opinion of the calling entirely plain. 'His name is Irwin.'

'Well,' said Williams, 'it will be interesting to have someone connected with the media among us. Perhaps we'll have to watch what we are doing or saying lest it ends up spread across the headlines.'

Mrs Jenkins pursed her lips, not at all sure whether this remark was a joke or a rebuke. Williams smiled—late.

'I understand he is divorced,' she said.

'I'm sorry to hear that. Divorce always wounds a person.'

'Do you mean, Minister, that you approve of divorce?'

'No, I don't. I believe in the sanctity of marriage, but if

someone comes into the community already divorced, we have to take him or her as we find them. We cannot undo what is done.'

'I see.' Glacially.

'I don't suppose you know when he is to move in? I will need to go and see him when he arrives.'

'I don't see that you do. But, as it happens, I do know that he is to move in on Thursday.'

'So soon?'

'I believe that the transaction took place some weeks ago.' Again from the tone, Williams gathered that it was improper of the parties to the sale to have proceeded without Mrs Jenkins's consent. They had not even had the courtesy to keep her informed!

2

So it was that Williams, driving past the Maxwells' old house in the middle of a rainy Thursday afternoon, saw that the furniture van which had been there in the morning had left. He stopped and rang the bell. Irwin came to the door in shirtsleeves. He had been unpacking.

'Yes?'

'Good afternoon. My name is Williams. I'm the local minister. I heard you were moving in, and when I saw the van had gone I thought I would ring the bell and welcome you to the village.'

'Humph.' Irwin stood irresolute, and then made a decision.

'You'd better come in. You'll get wet out there.' He led the way into the front room where an electric fire was doing its best to dispel the dampness which the shut-up room had accumulated.

'Can I offer you a drink?' he asked.

'No, thanks. I'm just passing. I'll come back some other time when it is more convenient.'

Irwin looked around at the packing cases and boxes scattered about the room. It was a bleak prospect.

'Well, perhaps that would be better. I'll have this place in shape by tomorrow. How about tomorrow evening?' He passed a weary hand over a sweaty brow.

'All right, if that suits you. But how would it be if I come and fetch you for something to eat later on today? You'll need something inside you, and some company is always nice in a new place.'

Irwin looked at Williams, focusing properly on him as an individual for the first time. Again he surveyed the room.

'All right,' he said slowly. 'All. Right. That might be good.'

'Fine,' said Williams. 'I'll go and organize it, and be back at, say . . .' He looked at his watch.

'Are you sure it won't be too much trouble for your wife?'

''Course not. We've often got—' he caught himself—'folk in at short notice.'

'Strays, you mean,' said Irwin shrewdly.

'Would six-thirty be all right?'

'Fine.'

Later that evening Irwin had mellowed in the warmth of hospitality.

'You know,' he said, 'I was not looking forward to the move down here. Strange place and all that. But you two —or four—' he included the children upstairs in a gesture —'have helped a lot.'

Ann smiled, comfortable and reassuring, as Irwin looked up, anxious lest he had shown too much of himself.

'Our pleasure,' she said.

'I expect you're wondering why I'm here,' went on Irwin. Neither Williams nor his wife said anything.

'It's just that I wanted to get away from the city life and down into a village like this. I was brought up in a village outside Edinburgh, and I suppose I'm going back into what I know.'

'They do say, never go back,' said Williams reflectively.

'I know. That's why I am coming here and not going back to my roots. But here I can remember my roots, and write.' This last admission seemed to have surprised Irwin. He stared at the fire.

'I'd have thought you got enough writing as it is,' said Ann.

'Not the right kind. Up at the *Gazette* it is a matter of speed, and reaction. Look at the wire-services. Listen to the radio. Go down to the courts. See the police. There's no time for reflection.'

'And I suppose also it is not the same as writing your own thoughts,' said Williams.

'No. There's always something.' Irwin fell silent.

'What are you going to write?' asked Ann. But before Irwin could reply Williams intervened.

'They say that you should never discuss such things. It takes the edge off writing.'

Irwin smiled. 'That's true. When I was down in London I used to come home of an evening and head off to the spare room and try to get some words down. But there was always a temptation to talk it out of my system by talking to Elsie.' His face clouded, but then he put memory behind him. 'Elsie was my wife. We broke up some years ago, in part because I was so busy trying to do a reporting job and to write a bestseller.'

'I'm sorry to hear that,' said Williams.

Irwin looked queerly at him, and then down at the fire again.

'You know, I believe you do mean that,' he said.

There was a brief silence.

'Well, the point is that I tried to tell Elsie what I was

doing . . . describe the story and such-like. And that just killed it. Killed it dead.'

'I can believe that,' said Williams. 'If I tell Ann the content of a sermon before I've got it down on paper it just goes out of the window.'

'Writing a book must be an awful effort,' said Ann.

Irwin laughed. 'I don't know,' he said. 'I've never managed to complete one yet. But I can tell you that half-writing a book is hell.' He went slightly red. 'Or do I mean purgatory?'

'Not in my denomination,' said Williams.

'Can you tell us what you are writing? Not the content but just the area. Is it a novel, or detective fiction, or what?'

'Don't laugh,' said Irwin. 'It seems to be turning into a romance, though it started as village life. I'll not say more than that.'

'Village life,' said Ann. 'You could write books and books about that.'

'But not publishable ones,' said Irwin. 'Think about PenIron here. I was on the scene not long after the police at the Hughes shooting. Now I bet there is a good story in that somewhere, and village life at the heart of it.'

Williams grunted, and then sighed.

'You're worried about the Hughes business, aren't you?'

'Perhaps.'

'Of course you are.' To Ann and Williams's surprise, Irwin got up and moved across to stand before the fire. Hands behind his back he rocked to and fro.

'It's a great bruise on the whole community,' said Williams.

'Look. You should leave all that to Alan Mason,' observed Irwin, still rocking backwards and forwards. 'If he can't do anything with the facts as they are, then no one can.'

'You think he is good?'

'As it happens, I know he is a friend of yours, but, yes, he is good.'

Williams let a flicker of surprise cross his face. He had not expected that Irwin would have that sort of knowledge.

Irwin grinned. 'It's my job.'

'What?'

'To know things. And especially about where I'm living, or going to live. Mason is someone I have come up against now and again. Bound to in reporting work. He's good.'

'But the police just don't seem to be getting anywhere,' said Williams.

'No. That's how it seems. But there is something about this case that doesn't feel right.'

'What do you mean?' said Ann anxiously.

'From what I hear there is some mystery about Hughes which they cannot straighten out.'

'You are a crime reporter, aren't you?' asked Ann.

Irwin nodded. 'I've been in and about it for many years, more years than I like to count. And this is an odd one.'

'Odd? It's disastrous,' said Williams.

'You're really worried about this thing, aren't you?' said Irwin.

Williams sighed.

'Yes, I am. It's like a cancer in the village. There's a distrust abroad in the streets. Everyone knows that someone has been killed, and that someone in the street may be the killer. It is most unsettling.'

'But it could well have been someone from elsewhere.'

'Logically, it could have been. But it seems to everyone that it is more likely to have been someone local. Even Alan Mason thinks that, I'm sure.'

'Has he said so?' The voice was quick.

Williams smiled. 'You won't get me that way. And if you print anything based on what I just said I'll be most upset.' His smile took the edge off the words, but Irwin saw he meant it.

'No, Minister. Of course not. But you'll not mind if I try to think things out myself, and grasp at any leads.'

Ann looked at Irwin, curious.

'Have you come here to solve the mystery?'

Irwin laughed. 'No, no. I arranged to buy the house some time ago, before the murder.'

'But you are hoping . . .?'

'Well, I suppose that were anything to come my way I would be stupid not to think about things, and perhaps help solve what happened. It is my profession, journalism, after all.'

'No offence meant,' said Ann, 'but I think that newspapers do stir up an awful lot just to sell papers.'

'Off the record,' replied Irwin, 'I agree. But I assure you I'm here really in a sort of partial retirement to see if I can write my book before it is all too late.'

'I was wondering about that,' said Williams. 'It does seem quite a way to commute to the *Greyhavens Gazette*.'

'I've an arrangement with the Editor. I've got a word-processor which can link me down the phone to the major wire services. I'll do three pieces for him a week, and he'll phone me if there is something special coming up that he wants to use me for. I'll write it up, and if necessary I can send my piece down the wire straight into his office.'

'The wonders of technology,' said Ann.

'Sounds quite nice,' said Williams. 'So you can enjoy your country life and get your book written.'

'Precisely. I live here and write, and still get paid enough to live on.'

'Do you have any children?' asked Ann.

'Yes,' replied Irwin, in a tone that forbade further discussion.

Again there was a silence. Irwin looked at the clock.

'Well,' he said, getting to his feet, 'if you don't mind I think I should be getting back.'

'Fair enough,' said Williams, also rising. 'I'll get your coat.' He left the room.

'How old are they?' said Ann.

Irwin pursed his lips. 'Sixteen, twelve and ten. Two boys and a girl,' he said.

Williams came back.

They drove in silence. At the house Irwin got out, turned and put his head in at the door.

'Thanks very much,' he said.

'Fine,' said Williams. 'I hope you settle soon.'

'You must come round some time and tell me a bit about the village,' said Irwin with a smile.

'Not much to it.'

'Llareggub.'

'He drank himself to death.'

Irwin looked straight at Williams. 'Good night,' he said.

SEVEN: AUGUST

1

The rest of June saw no progress on the matter of the death of Evan Hughes. Nor did it seem to see any progress within the life of the village. To Williams it was as if there was a pall hanging over the place. The weather was good, better than it had been for some years. One of his parishioners who kept meteorological records proclaimed towards the end of the month that it had been the sunniest June in PenIron for forty-three years, but Williams felt that he must have got his figures wrong.

The gloom made its way into his preaching.

Ann kept silence, hoping that their coming holiday would provide a lift which would get her husband out of the spiral he seemed to be in. But July and the holiday did not seem to help.

As an experiment and on the advice of a friend they had taken a cottage on the west coast, and as a holiday it was marvellous. All of them got burned on the smooth silver sands. Paul and Williams fished happily for sea trout of an evening from the small boat which went with the house. Ann got a lot of reading done, and was happy just to potter about. Not to have a phone ring was in itself a major element in the vacation. The only news that Peter Wade thought worth bothering them with was the death of old Mrs Fletcher. She had rallied a little, getting her speech back, but then had died peacefully one night. Ian Paterson at Linxton had been asked to take the funeral.

So it was a good and relaxing holiday. But, as they drove

back to PenIron at the end of the month, Ann could see the gloom descend once more on her husband.

2

The news of their return soon got round the village, and various people came to call. One of these was Jessie Munro.

'Mrs Fletcher asked me to give you this,' she said, thrusting a large Victorian picture album into Williams's hands.

Later that afternoon, he sat with Ann and looked through it. It had been beautifully kept, with neat letters indicating the content of each and every picture.

The phone rang.

'It's all right,' he said. 'The machine's on. Let's just leave it to talk to whoever it is.'

As she turned the pages, Ann stopped suddenly and tapped one with her finger. She read the inscription and looked up at Williams.

'Look at that,' she said. 'It's Evan Hughes, just like Alan said.'

Williams looked. The figure was dressed in casual flannels, and did indeed look like Hughes.

'Look at the eyes and nose,' she breathed. 'That's what old Isaac meant the day of the funeral. I bet if we were to look into things we would find that Donald Anthony had a reputation like Hughes did. He was following in his father's footsteps.'

Williams nodded. He turned the pages on. There were one or two other pictures of Donald Anthony, and the resemblance was even clearer.

Ann got up and moved over to the window, where she stood a moment in thought.

'How old was Harold Anthony?' she asked.

'I can't remember. About twenty-one or twenty-two, I suppose.'

'And Donald was younger or older than our Miss Anthony?'

'Younger, I think. By about two years I think she said to me once.'

'And he died—what was it? Four or five years ago?'

'Something like that.'

'And Miss Anthony was what when she died?'

'Eighty-six.'

Ann did some sums in her head, and then turned with a slight smile.

'So the old goat must have been sixty-one or -two when Harold was born.'

Williams shrugged his shoulders.

'It must run in the family,' went on Ann. 'If he had to go to Australia because he had tripped over the traces, it might be that Evan Hughes was that trip. That's what Isaac meant by saying to work out the dates. Like father, like son.'

Then she saw that her husband's shoulders had slumped. The book lay unheeded in his lap.

'I'm sorry, dear,' she said. 'I didn't mean to bring it all back. It's all past now. Alan has done his best, and we must just get on despite it all.'

'No,' he said, with a sigh. 'No, it's not like that. There is truth in the Old Testament principle. When blood has been shed near a village it has to be atoned for. The blood-guilt does mean something. Haven't you seen how the place has been affected?'

'I've seen how it has affected you,' she said fiercely, sitting down beside him and taking his hands. 'You mustn't let it get to you. It's affected everything you do. It is not good for the people. They'll start not coming to church if it is gloom and doom every Sunday.'

'I can't help it. That is what is there in the Book.'

She shook her head. 'I think you'd better go and have a

word with someone about it. I hoped the holiday would get things into perspective, but it doesn't seem really to have helped if you're going to get down about it all almost as soon as we are through the door.'

'I know,' he said.

'Oh, go play with your trains or something,' she said with sudden anger. This passivity was not something she knew how to cope with.

As she left, he turned again to the photographs. There was no doubt about the link. The eyes. The high nose. Miss Anthony had had that too. Even if Mason had not told him back in May, he would have known that Donald Anthony and Evan Hughes came from the same stock.

He felt something deep within him settle into place. He didn't know what, but a step had been taken.

Ann heard him whistling as he made his way upstairs to Williamston. She was pleased. Somehow she had hit the right button, she thought.

3

Next morning Ann glanced at her husband as he came back into the kitchen.

'What's wrong?' she asked.

He grinned sheepishly at her. 'Nothing really, I suppose. Miss Andrews is back.'

'Oh!' she said, with a *moue* of exasperation.

'There was only the one call on the box. I phoned her back. I'm afraid she is coming round. There's something on her mind.'

'There is nothing on her mind at all. I'm sure one day when I was in church and she was sitting against the light, I could see right through from ear to ear.'

He laughed.

'It's true,' she said. 'She's an empty-headed gossip who's got a fixation on her minister. I expect that somehow or other you remind her of some favourite pupil or other. She takes liberties with you that I bet she never took with Dr Jones.'

'I would hope not,' said Williams, still smiling. 'He was old enough to have been her grandfather. Still, it isn't often she phones. Usually she lies in wait for me after services.' He mimed a prowling cat.

'That's true, I suppose,' said Ann. 'But I was hoping you would help me with the spare room.'

'Ah,' said Williams. 'Now we have it. The drudge is escaping. That's what is wrong. God bless Miss Andrews.'

'When is she coming?'

'Eleven-fifteen.'

'That gives us over an hour.'

'But that's coffee-time.'

'Not today it's not. You can have coffee with Miss Andrews.'

The bell rang at the worst possible moment. The two were trying not very successfully to ease a wardrobe through the spare room door.

'Oh no,' said Ann. 'I forgot about the Andrews.'

'So did I,' said Williams. 'Quick. Maybe we've got it right this time.' Moments later he grimaced as his knuckles once again scraped the door-frame.

'No good,' he said. 'Take it back. We'll just have to try again later.'

They moved the wardrobe out again into the passage, and set it down, upright once more. With difficulty Williams eased his way between the wardrobe and the banister.

'No,' said Ann. 'You'd better go and wash. I'll let her in and explain.'

He looked at his hand where dark blood was welling from

what had seemed a white scrape. He nodded, and went back past the wardrobe.

Ann scampered down the stairs, shedding her smock on the way.

Moments later, as he ran water over his hand, Williams heard her showing Miss Andrews into the study. He looked at himself in the mirror. He was tousled, hot and dirty.

Well, Ann could cope. He reached for the soap.

It was five or so minutes later that the Reverend Edward Williams entered his study to meet one of the highly respected ladies of his congregation. That, at least was the impression he gave. He saw a twinkle in Ann's eye as she took in the alteration from the recent past. Even his tie matched his shirt.

'Do you think we could have coffee?' he asked urbanely as she left.

She showed more than the tip of her tongue, and he turned quickly. Miss Andrews was looking out at the window.

4

'But really,' continued Miss Andrews some time later, 'I did not come here to waste your time. It is so good, however, to talk to someone who does appreciate the finer things of life, and the Turners at the Tate are so magnificent, so magnificent.'

'Not at all,' said Williams, with a forced geniality. 'But you did say that there was something particularly on your mind.'

'Ah yes,' said Miss Andrews, drawing herself together and looking rather prim. She picked up her handbag and put it on her lap and crossed her hands on top of it. 'I'm

not actually entirely sure, now that I am talking to you . . .
but it is my duty . . .'

Williams's heart sank. He had heard this gambit before.
It usually spelled trouble.

'I was staying, as you know, with my sister at Tring. Such
a lovely little place, apart from the awful new building going
on round it. A wonderful church in the middle. It does us
Presbyterians so much good occasionally to attend other
places of worship, and the Tring church is wonderful. Wonderful.'

She caught something of his impatience.

'Well. To the point. On Thursday last, Mavis and I had
decided to get an early train into London. It is so difficult,
you know. There are so many commuters nowadays from
so far out. Not as it was when Mavis and Henry went there
thirty years ago. There are more trains, but now they are
so busy. So busy.

'Henry ran us to the station, and we didn't have long to
wait. We took the express in, the one that doesn't stop
between Watford and Harrow and Wealdstone.

'It is such a lovely ride, you know. There is the Union
Canal wending its way through the countryside. And just
outside Berkhamsted there is the most wonderful view of
the old castle—Norman, I think it was, with a moat—the
view from the train is far better than anything you can get
from the ground. Yes, it must be Norman. Berkhamsted is
where William received the surrender of London in 1066.
Unfortunately there is a modernish bungalow inside the
walls now. Whoever put it in has tried to make it seemly; it
is in a sort of Tudor style, with brown tiling and the right
sort of pitched roofs and windows. But it is intrusive none
the less. Still, if you forget that, you can see how extensive
and important the castle must have been at one time.'

Williams felt his interested smile congealing on his lips,
but he said nothing. As he well knew from many encounters,
Miss Andrews had been an enthusiastic History teacher.

He found himself wondering how many pupils she had thoroughly sickened of the subject, and then mentally rebuked himself. The evidence was that she had taught a number who had gone on into History themselves. She must have passed on her interest. He dragged his attention back. Miss Andrews pressed on.

'As it happened on that trip I sat with my back to the engine, and Mavis was sitting opposite me. When we got to Harrow I saw someone I recognized. I was just going to wave when I saw he was with some . . . some person. Fortunately I did nothing. I think perhaps I turned my head. At any rate I don't think he recognized me.'

'He?' inquired Williams.

'Just wait,' said Miss Andrews, turned teachery. 'You had better hear the rest first.

'When we got into Euston, I made some excuse and delayed Mavis so that they would have gone, so we came out towards the end of the passengers. And there were so many. So many.

'But he was there, standing just where the ramp goes up to the main station concourse and the tunnel goes on down to the Underground, between platforms eleven and twelve.'

Williams moved himself. Where was this leading?

'They were embracing.' Miss Andrews coloured, and searched in her handbag for a handkerchief.

'I am not really sure . . .' began Williams.

'But you must,' interrupted Miss Andrews. 'It was Peter Wade, the Session Clerk. The girl—well, I suppose she must have been in her late twenties—she was all over him. It was most unseemly. A quite unsuitable . . . fur jacket and leather skirt.' She sniffed.

Williams slumped to release the tension he felt.

'But you cannot be certain . . .'

'Oh yes I can,' said Miss Andrews. 'I have sat near Peter Wade in church for many years, and I could not be wrong

on that. Besides, he walked like him as he went up the ramp.
She went down to the Tube.'

'And he didn't see you?'

'No. At least if he did, he didn't indicate it.'

'And you didn't say hello? After all you could have been
mistaken and that would have cleared matters up.'

'I could hardly have done that, could I? It was all so
unseemly.'

'No. No, when you put it like that I suppose you couldn't
have said anything.' Williams dismissed his suggestion with
a wave. He almost smiled, and then recollected himself.

'Maybe she was an old friend,' he ventured.

'Old friend.' The tone was glacial. 'They came on to that
train, that *early* train, hand in hand, and then carried on
like . . . like . . .' She sputtered to a halt.

'Well,' said Williams rising to his feet. 'Thank you for
telling me all this. I am not sure what to make of it.'

Miss Andrews also rose.

'As I said, I felt it was my duty to bring the matter to
your attention.'

'I think it would be best if nothing were said about this
. . . this "problem", for a while. Just until I can think things
out and get things clear in my mind,' said Williams. 'I'll
need to decide how to handle it.'

'My lips are sealed,' said Miss Andrews. 'You know I am
the soul of discretion. I would not have mentioned it even
to you, except that you are the minister and he is an
office-bearer in the congregation.'

'Yes. Yes, I know you are,' replied Williams, his thoughts
being quite the reverse. 'You felt it was your duty.'

'Quite.'

He watched her go down the drive. As he expected, she
turned right when she got to the road.

'She'll be off to see Mrs Jenkins,' he thought gloomily.

5

Late August turned unseasonably rainy, making the grouse-shooting dismal.

'I'm told it's no good this year,' said Colin Marsh one day when he met Williams in the street. 'With Miss Anthony's death, the estate hasn't got round to appointing a gamekeeper to take Hughes's job, and in any event there's not many birds this year.'

Friday night was Williams's vestry night. It had been the time set aside by his predecessor. When he had come to PenIron Williams had balked at the idea of a fixed 'vestry', being of the opinion that he ought to be available to any of his flock at any time. But he never got round to changing the tradition and in fact soon found himself looking forward to it. There were some nights on which there were no visitors, and then he would read a book for the half-hour before making his way back home to the manse. On others there would be several people to be seen, and many problems to be listened to. From these other opportunities could come.

The only problem was heating. Williams (and the Treasurer) felt it unnecessary to have the central heating in the church turned on for a mere thirty minutes' use of a part of the building. For safety reasons he was reluctant to call in and put on an electrical radiator specially in the afternoon. The result was that for most of the year the temperature in the vestry never really dispelled the accumulated dampness and chill of the rest of the week. However, if he wrapped up well . . .

He got there early, put on the electric fire and settled

down with a travel book on Central America. One of these days, he always hoped, he would be able to go and see those magnificent monuments for himself.

About twenty past seven, as the cold was beginning to get to him, he heard shuffling footsteps outside the vestry and then a knock at the door.

It was a couple who, he knew, had moved into one of the cottages out on the Linxton road a couple of years previously. They had never been in when he had gone to welcome them to the village, and had ignored his written invitation to church or to get in touch if he or Ann could be any help in their settling in. He thought there had been a baby recently. The woman was quite attractive with long brown hair. The man, nondescript.

They came into the vestry, the woman somewhat boldly, Williams thought. The man, thin and intense, came in looking around, but not at Williams.

The woman came straight to the point after she had sat down, and before Williams could ask their name.

'We've come to see about having the child baptized,' she said abruptly.

'I see,' replied Williams, getting a sheet of paper from his desk drawer and taking out his pen.

'I take it that you do understand what is meant by baptism?' he asked.

The woman looked puzzled. 'We've come to have the child done,' she replied. 'You are the parish minister, aren't you?'

'Indeed I am. But I must be sure that you know what you are doing. It is not just a question of giving the child a name. The parents, and the congregation, take very serious vows about the way the child will be reared. It is a matter of offering the child back to God in a way.'

'The name will be Jocelyn.'

Williams laid his pen down. 'I don't think you understood me,' he said. 'Baptism is for the children of believers, or in some cases others can take the vows for the child. You are not members here, are you?'

The man got to his feet. 'That's it, is it?' he asked. He turned to the woman. 'I told you, Sue. This place is not for us.'

He turned back to Williams. 'No,' he said. 'We're not members here. Nor are we married. We don't think that love has anything to do with a few words spoken by a man dressed up in a black sheet.'

'Neither do I,' responded Williams, to the man's great surprise. 'There is a lot more to it than that.'

The result was a longish, interesting discussion, which ended with the pair inviting Williams to come round and visit some evening when he was free. Clearly the matter of the baptism could wait.

'Kidd's the name,' said the man as they left. 'Melvin Kidd.'

Williams locked up and left after them. The car's heater did nothing to help. Nor really did the tea which Ann made as soon as he appeared. It was not until he had been a while under the electric blanket that he began to feel really comfortable.

6

It was 'flu, and a nasty dose at that. A student from Greyhavens took the Sunday services while Williams sweated and ached. On the Wednesday afternoon he got downstairs for an hour or so, and more on the Thursday.

On Friday, Mason came visiting.

'You've had a time of it, I hear,' he said as he sat down opposite Williams in the study.

'So I'm told. But I'm feeling a lot better now.'

Mason looked surreptitiously at him. Ann had said that

Williams was a lot stronger, but Mason was not so sure. His friend had that transparent look to his hand that comes of much sweating and bed-rest.

'Well, I was passing, and when I phoned the other day to ask how you were, Ann said you would be visible soon. So as I was passing today I thought I'd see for myself.'

'That's good of you. It does get a little boring after a day or so, when you're beginning to feel better.'

'I hear you collapsed and fell out of the pulpit!'

Williams grinned. 'I'm sure Peter Wade thought it was a judgement.'

'Like his car accident?'

'Perhaps. You folk never found anything out about that?'

'No. I thought you and he got on all right.'

'Oh, we get on all right, but I suspect he would be quite pleased if I moved on, or out into the graveyard.'

'What makes you say that?'

'I'm not really sure. It's just a feeling. Sometimes I think that the preaching gets under his skin. A more comfortable, traditional sermon—blessed thoughts and not too many of those, is what he'd like.'

Mason laughed. 'You've been stirring his conscience?'

'Well, I don't know about that. But just sometimes . . . I believe he had old Dr Jones under his thumb, really. He thought being nice to people was the whole of the gospel.'

'That doesn't sound like the Peter Wade that I know.'

'I was talking about Jones. No. Peter is more of a traditionalist. I think he comes to church because that is the thing which the local rich man ought to do. I'm sure he enjoys being Session Clerk.'

Mason rubbed the side of his nose briefly. Williams, who had been reading *Man-watching*, viewed the gesture with interest.

'My impression,' said Mason carefully, 'is that Wade has been having financial trouble these past few years. He moved out of criminal work, yet his property business hasn't been that lucrative, I wouldn't have thought. One just hears the odd whisper.'

'He runs a nice Mercedes.'

'I know.'

The two sat silent for a minute or so.

'He does all the legal work for the PenIron Estate,' ventured Williams.

'That can't be all that much.'

'Well, there was Miss Anthony's personal work as well. I believe from something she said that he had a power of attorney there in latter years.'

Mason shrugged. 'Ah well,' he said, getting to his feet. 'Give me a salary with the credit of a local authority at the back of it any day. I couldn't live with the uncertainties of the business world nowadays. Or ever!'

'Must you go? I've been thinking out some modifications to the track upstairs, and I'd like your opinion on them,' said Williams, also rising.

'Ah! Have you? Are you conceding that that signal box in the far corner is quite anachronistic for 1914?'

'Rubbish. I've shown you the photographic evidence for it.'

'And I've told you that the photo is misdated.'

Ann heard them arguing as Williams showed Mason out. Clearly her husband was well on the way to recovery.

EIGHT: SEPTEMBER

1

By the time they were well into September, Ann was close to losing her patience again. Perhaps it was the 'flu, but Williams's mood was swinging backwards and forwards. All would seem to be well until something would remind him of the Hughes affair, and after that he would be in a blue mood for at least a day. Somehow or other it always seemed to strike him at the time for preparing the Sunday sermons, irrespective when in the week he tried to get down to it.

And the preaching suffered. She even encountered comment on that from non-church members when she went shopping in the village.

'A right Hell-fire man your husband's turned into by all accounts,' was one of the remarks made to her out of the blue. One member phoned her when she knew Williams would be out, just to explain that she had had enough, and would come back when she heard that the preaching had changed. She and Ann had been friendly, and she just wanted to explain her absence, though Ann, of course, had not to mention this to her husband.

One Monday towards the end of the month she was getting very worried. Williams and his friend Duncan Raeburn were upstairs working on the model railway, when she saw something interesting in the newspaper. She folded it and took it upstairs.

'Do you really mean,' said Williams, quite disconcerted when she showed it to him, 'that you are proposing that Duncan and I go on a railway outing? Are you feeling all

right, woman. You usually grumble at anything remotely
like such a suggestion.'

'You go,' said Ann firmly. 'It will do you good. Won't it,
Duncan?'

Duncan was examining the advertisement.

'Yes,' he said. 'Come on, man. Never look a gift horse in
the mouth. The trip is the end of next week.'

2

Williams was late for the train. As Ann dropped him in the
station yard at Birley he could see it was already in. He
made it on to the platform as the guard was blowing his
whistle, and dived into the carriage opposite the station
entrance. He paused to catch his breath, and then made his
way forward. Duncan always sat in the first coach if he
could. According to him, that way he got there before
everyone else. In fact, it usually meant that he was well-
placed for the buffet car.

Duncan was not on the train.

Williams snorted, and settled down in a corner. For some
reason he felt out of sorts; too out of sorts really to enjoy the
passing scenery. He prodded his overnight bag. No, there
was no book in there. Ann had expected him to look after
that side of things himself.

He gave himself up to brooding, only absently acknowledging the various things which would usually have de-
lighted him, the timbered signal boxes and the remains of
spur lines.

He dozed lightly, then woke. The train was climbing at
one side of the valley. Over on the other side he saw the
stream of cars on the new A74, and above it the line of the
old road wending its way.

His mind went back into its familiar rut. There was a

sickness in the parish, he thought. Something was sapping
the life of the place. The Hughes murder lay like a blanket
of fog across what had been a happy community. That and
the attempt on Peter Wade's life. He prayed briefly as he
watched the traffic on the road. Two lorries were grinding
up a steep section, collecting cars in their train. That'll slow
them down, he thought. Justifies the train.

He looked at his watch. Two and a bit hours. It was over
three hours to Carlisle. How long would it have taken by
car? Behind those lorries it would have taken an age. And
of course he would be fresh when he arrived—or so the
advertising claimed. How long would the car have taken?

At Carlisle he got off, and phoned home. Duncan had
been in touch. Something or other had detained him, and
he was coming on the next train down.

Williams went into the station buffet and had a sandwich.
Then he checked the time of the Settle train. There was still
about an hour to wait before Duncan would arrive, so he
went for a stroll.

Outside the station he saw a sign for a car hire company.
'The Do-it-Yourself Way', it said in bright yellow letters on
a black background.

A sudden thought niggled.

He walked around briefly, praying. Should he, or
shouldn't he? There was no flash of inspiration: he didn't
expect there to be. He sat on a bench and thought the thing
out. There was nothing to lose. Someone might laugh at
him, but that would be all. Even if there was a com-
plaint . . . ? But that was unlikely. If his inquiry were re-
pulsed, then so be it. If not, then at least one avenue would
have proved empty.

3

'I really oughtn't to be doing this,' said the man, straightening up with a large box file in his hand.

'I really am most grateful to you,' said Williams. 'And it is important. It will settle something which is troubling a number of people.'

The man still looked doubtful, but dumped the box on his desk and opened it up. 'April, you said?' he asked.

'Yes. I would think that it would be April twenty-third, -fourth or -fifth. The Friday perhaps.'

The man nodded, riffling through the contents of the file. Then he grunted.

'What name?'

Williams gave a name.

'Yes. That's right. There was a hire on Friday the twenty-fourth to someone called that.' The man appeared to relax. There was something to this odd question he had been asked, after all. He shut the box file and leaned forward, his hand on it, looking keenly at Williams.

'Could I see it?'

'Well . . .' said the man. 'I'm not sure that I should let you see anything. You've not told me why you are wanting to know. I'm sure the boss wouldn't like it.'

Williams sat down at the other side of the desk. The man stood, looking at him.

'It has something to do with a member of my congregation,' said Williams at last.

'But how do I know that?' asked the man. 'I don't even know that you are a minister. You don't look like one. You aren't dressed right.'

Williams glanced down at himself and laughed.

'I don't suppose I do,' he said. 'I'm not here really to

come in and ask. It was just an impulse when I saw your firm here close to the station.

'I can show you my driving licence and cheque-book. I think that the cheque-book has me down as "Rev". But I was just here to have a ride with a friend on the Settle line. We are railway buffs. I came down earlier than he could manage, so I have an hour or so to wait. I was going to look around the station, because it has been some years since I was here last. But I saw your sign, and . . .' He shrugged.

'OK,' said the man. 'That is really all I wanted to know. If you had taken what I said as a hint I wanted to be paid, you'd have got no further. If you were a private detective you would have had said so long ago. As it is, here you are.' He slid the box across the desk, and sat down.

'Thanks,' said Williams, and looked at the documents. About one-third of the way through he slowed up and stared.

There was a car hire form in a familiar surname for April 24th. The forename was different and the address given was Walthamstow, London. The signature was not very like that one which Williams had grown familiar with, though there were resemblances in the flowing capitals.

He sighed.

'No help?' said the man, studying him.

'I don't know,' replied Williams. 'It might be, or it might not be. I just don't know.' He replaced the material and pushed the box back across the desk.

'How do you get the data?' he asked.

'Off the Driving Licence, usually. Though with these long-dated licences nowadays the addresses are often quite different. Makes no sense to put on an address when the licence is to be valid until the holder is seventy, does it? Stupid, I call it.'

'How long do you keep the forms?' Williams asked.

'Only until the accountants have been through the audit.'

'Oh. How long will that be?' Williams asked.

'About another month.'

Williams thought furiously.

As he did so the man opened the box again, and riffled through the carbons. 'What one interested you?' he asked.

'Twenty-fourth April,' said Williams. 'The Renault.'

The man pulled out the form. He scanned it. 'You know,' he said, 'I think I remember this one. Yes. I think I remember this one. It was odd. Paid for in cash. See the box.' He pointed at a check-box at the bottom left-hand corner of the form.

'That's unusual, is it?' said Williams.

'It is nowadays. Usually there is a cheque, or most often a credit card.'

'So why would he have paid in cash?'

'Dunno,' said the man, relaxing into a smile. 'I expect he didn't want to be traced. Maybe it was untaxed income. Or maybe his wife pays off the credit card each month and would be suspicious at an entry for car hire, especially if there was a hotel bill for two as well.' He almost broke into a leer, and then straightened his face abruptly as he remembered the company he was in.

'But you remember him?'

'Sort of. Sort of.'

Williams looked his question.

'He was an ordinary sort of guy. Sports jacket, if I remember right. Nothing special.'

'No luggage?'

'Don't remember none.'

'Would you remember which train he came off?'

'Not really. I suppose we could work it out from the form.' He looked at it.

'See,' he said, pointing. 'The hire was half past two. That looks like the London train, to me. It gets in at 2.10. But it could as easily be the 2.20 from the North. None of those keep the times, you know.'

Williams smiled. 'And when did the car come back?'

'Five the next day.' The man stopped, tapping his finger

on the form. 'That reminds me of something else. As I remember, he wanted all the copies of the hire form, but I wouldn't let him have them. He was quite upset.'

Williams raised his eyebrows.

'I was new here as manager, then,' explained the man defensively. 'My predecessor was fired for pilfering. All these forms are numbered, see. If someone spotted that there was one missing from the sequence, they might think I had done the same.'

'Even if you could show cash receipts?'

'They wouldn't have shown what the hire figure should have been.'

Williams nodded. The point was good. Then he added, 'I suppose that that means that I can't take this one away.'

'Right,' said the man.

'And I don't suppose you have a photocopier.'

'No,' said the man.

Williams thought briefly.

'Are there any photocopiers anywhere near here?' he asked.

'There's a fast-copy shop round the corner,' replied the man. 'But . . .'

His voice trailed away as Williams took out his wallet and his cheque-book out of his pocket, put them on the desk, and then added his watch to the heap.

'Look,' said Williams, 'you keep your eyes on these for a couple of minutes and let me dash round the corner with that form.'

'You some kind of nut?' asked the man.

'Sort of,' said Williams.

'All right,' said the man suddenly. A new theory had struck him. He leaned back in his chair expansively. 'Where have you got the cameras hidden?' He looked around. 'This is one of those daft set-ups, isn't it? Who put you up to it? My wife? Barney? What programme are you? What TV channel are you from?'

'I'm serious,' said Williams seriously. 'It could be very important.'

The man straightened up and looked carefully at Williams. Then he took a deep breath. 'They'll never believe this at the pub tonight,' he said.

'I would hope you wouldn't say anything about it to anyone,' replied Williams.

'OK, OK,' said the man, capitulating. 'Here you are.' He passed over the form. 'Just be back before we shut.'

'Don't know what's got into him,' said Duncan, as Ann collected Williams when they returned. Ann looked at her husband. There was an air of suppressed excitement about him. Had the break done him good? she wondered.

4

In the morning Williams could not settle to work.

'What's wrong with you?' asked Ann as he again prowled into the kitchen.

'Nothing. Nothing,' he said, and went back out again.

Three or four minutes later he came back, this time looking for coffee. Ann, who knew a difficult sermon in preparation when she saw it, did not ask again, but filled the minutes while the kettle was boiling with speculation about the changes that were to happen in the staffing at the local primary school. A well-loved older teacher was retiring, and there was speculation that they would instead get someone long on 'projects' but short on the three 'R's'.

Williams paid no attention, took his coffee and wandered back to the study. There was a double sheet of A4 paper in front of him, but though at first sight it was laid out much as his normal sermon preparation, closer scrutiny would have shown that the different headings had little to do with either Testament, and the inked and pencilled lines between different items did not carry strands of theological thought. It looked like a plan for model railway sidings.

He sat looking at the sheet for a minute. Then he took up a red felt pen, and with it traced out one set of the linking lines. Here and there he added a large flowing question-mark. Then he sat back and looked at it once more.

Then he picked up his phone.

'Alan,' said Williams abruptly, when he got through to Mason. 'Would you answer me a question, even if it is improper?'

'Depends,' came his friend's voice. 'Try me.'

'The Anthony post-mortem. I was wondering if the shot had balled.'

There was a distinct pause at the other end of the line.

'That would be quite out of order,' said Mason at length. 'And in any case I wouldn't know. I didn't deal with it. It was Albert Gilchrist who carried out that investigation.'

'Oh well,' said Williams. 'It was just a thought.'

He put the phone down, and then cleared the papers off his desk. There had to be a sermon for Sunday, but the thoughts came with great difficulty.

5

'Come in. Come in, Minister,' Irwin said that evening, hospitable in form even if his smile did not reach his eyes.

Williams did not apologize or make any excuses. He wanted to talk to Irwin, and was not going to provide him with any chink which would allow him to indicate that Williams was unwelcome or that he should go. Williams had business to settle in his own mind.

Irwin took him into a very correct front room. It was

cold, and obviously unlived in. Williams looked aound and took the bull by the horns.

'Look,' he said, 'I'm sorry. I've got very important things to ask you and it would be best if things were as informal as possible, otherwise I'm going to freeze up.'

Irwin straightened up from where he was just switching on the electric fire. He glanced shrewdly at Williams and then bent down and put the fire off again.

'Come on through.' He gestured to the door. Clearly he was puzzled. Was this minister going to treat him as a confessional? Other men had in their time, when he was . . . He shied away from that train of thought.

In the back room Irwin cleared off a chair for Williams and settled into his own armchair on the other side of the fire. There was a smell of burning wood, probably from the fire.

Williams looked round. The room was comfortable in a curiously detached sort of way. There was a bookcase on the wall facing him, neatly arranged he could see at a glance. Other things were less well cared for. On top of the sideboard were pictures of three children.

Irwin followed his eyes, and then turned to poke the fire. He added some lumps of coal from a brass coal-scuttle, and swithered about putting on a log as well from a pile beside it. When he had finished, he carefully pushed the poker into the coals.

'Well?'

Williams began carefully.

'I understand that at one time you were employed down in London.'

Irwin snorted. 'I was the best they had.'

'So I gather.'

'Checking, have you been?'

'No, not at all, but when I was younger I can remember your by-line on stories.'

'So? That's a long time ago now.' Irwin's eyes went to

the photographs on the sideboard. His face softened and then hardened.

'In London, I believe it is possible . . .' Williams broke off, and started again. 'No. First I must ask you for an assurance that whatever I might say to you, or whatever you may deduce from anything I might say, will remain strictly private and confidential. No one must know. Nothing must be said, written or printed. Nothing at all.'

Irwin chuckled. 'What's up, Padre? Are you running off with the cash and the Treasurer's wife?'

Williams was not sure how the pleasantry was meant, and showed his bewilderment.

Irwin immediately relented.

'Sorry, I couldn't resist the thrust. You looked so solemn and guilty just now. But I can't give that sort of assurance cold. Tell me why I should.'

Williams sat for a moment, ordering his thoughts. A large part of him regretted having come, yet perhaps this was the only way, short of going to Alan Mason, which would have been impossible. Who else did he know who might have the sort of information he needed? No one.

He sighed.

'I need your promise of confidentiality for two reasons. First, because I am a minister and in speaking to you— asking for your help—I am, as it were, deputizing you.' A pure childlike smile broke over his face. 'Yes. Just like in those Wild West movies we saw when we were young. I am deputizing you.'

'Now wait a moment, Reverend . . .' began Irwin, but Williams waved him silent.

'I am deputizing you into the pastoral care of the community you have chosen to come and live in. You can help me. And we all need that help. We have a community problem.'

Irwin relaxed again. 'You have a problem community,' he said.

'I know what I said,' responded Williams. 'I know what you mean, but that is a long-term job. There is an immediate problem, however. Can I have your word of honour?'

To his astonishment Irwin started to laugh.

He waited. Irwin subsided.

'I'm sorry,' said Irwin, still chuckling. 'I thought you were here, perhaps, to call in my promise to come to church one of these days, and you talk to me of honour. My honour.' He sobered. 'I am here, a failure. I was a good reporter down in London. Too good. I nerved myself for it by drink. I lost everything and now here I am back where I started twenty-five years ago as a reporter, and occasionally as a stringer for London.'

It was his turn to wave Williams to silence.

'My marriage has gone. I haven't seen my children for years. I sometimes go back down to London and walk. Walk in the hope that I'll see one or other of them in the street. In the street! And you want me to help you solve a community problem, by the sound of it, in absolute secrecy.'

As he spoke the last sentence he leaned forward to look closely at Williams.

'All right.' He stopped abruptly. 'All right. What can I do for you? In complete secrecy.'

Williams clasped his hands and looked down at them.

'If I wanted a gun, how would I go about getting it?'

Irwin looked at him sharply. Then he got up and walked about, coming to a halt in front of the fire.

'I was wondering,' said Williams, 'if I wanted to get my hands on a shotgun, how I would go about it.'

Irwin glanced at him shrewdly.

'Thinking of getting rid of the wife, are you? Or is it just that the pigeons are getting too much of the peas in the garden?' he asked.

'Just suppose,' returned Williams blandly.

'Well, if it is the pigeons that are the trouble, I imagine that you should just have a word with almost any one of

your parishioners. And if they can't help, come back to me,
for I've a gun in the front cupboard.'

Williams smiled. 'And if it is a matter of the wife?'

Irwin frowned.

'That's not funny,' he said abruptly.

Williams cursed himself. Interested in his own thoughts
he had forgotten Irwin's marital situation. But the cloud
passed.

'A shotgun.' Irwin mused. 'Are you serious?'

'Yes.'

Irwin paced about again, while Williams waited. Then
he sat down.

'I take it it is not for personal use?'

Williams smiled and shook his head.

'Well, there are guns and guns. You could get one from
a gunshop. Then you'd need to get it licensed. Do I gather
you would be wanting it illicitly?'

Williams nodded.

'A pistol? You could get that easy enough in most big
cities.'

Williams shook his head slowly.

'A shotgun, you would be better to get somewhere big.'

Williams was still. Irwin sat down opposite him.

'You're after whoever shot Evan Hughes.'

Williams said nothing, but looked into the fire. The poker
end was almost white.

Irwin followed his gaze. He took the poker out of the fire,
and picked up a slab of wood which was lying on top of the
pile of logs. He put the slab on the tiles beside him, and
started to pick out a picture with the hot poker. While he
did this he spoke slowly.

'If it is a matter of a person, you would be best either
with a rifle if it is long-range, or a pistol for short-range
work. But the best of all would be a sawn-off shotgun. You
could keep it concealed under your coat until you need it,
and yet it has such a wide spread of shot that you would

not need to be too accurate in your shooting. Unlike a gun.'

'And if I wanted to get a sawn-off shotgun?'

'If I were after a sawn-off shotgun I would get it down in London. There are several pubs and places where you could quite easily get on the track of one. It might take a little time, but you can do it. You go into some of the sleazier areas, and into a pub or two. Do that a few times, and then you start asking one or two questions—giving hints and the like. Someone would get in touch with you then. The beauty of London is that most of the stuff is untraceable by the time it gets there.'

He was working on a brief sketch of a sun sinking into a sea in a small bay.

Williams was fascinated, but persevered with his own line of thought.

'Why not go to Newcastle, or Glasgow or Manchester?'

'Those are all possible too. But London is the safest. It would have the advantage of not remembering at all.'

'Not even if Mason is asking the questions?'

'Especially so. Never remember anything for the police.'

'Why not?'

'It's a good habit to have.'

'And what about reporters?'

Irwin laughed. 'I've had a few good tips out of men in pubs. Then again the one real beating I've had also came as a result of asking questions.'

Williams fell silent.

When Irwin was finished his poker-work, Williams said, 'That is what I thought too.'

Irwin hefted the poker once or twice, and then put it back in the fire.

'What I can't work out,' said Williams slowly, 'is where the gun went afterwards, and why it happened at all.'

Irwin leaned back into his chair.

'It happened,' said Irwin, 'because he had it coming to him.' He chuckled. 'Think of it as a post-natal abortion.'

Williams shook his head. 'No,' he replied. 'I'm not anti capital punishment, but not for a case like Hughes.'

'Why not?' asked Irwin. 'The trouble with our law in general is that it is only concerned with what a man does, not with what he is. That's one thing the Soviets have got right in theory, if not in practice. They are concerned with what a criminal is, above and beyond what the man has done.'

'No. A man is punished for what he does.'

'Surely, Minister, at the last judgement what a man *is* is more important than what he has done. That's why the whores are going to go into the Kingdom and the pharisees are going to be left out.'

Williams smiled. 'We'll need to talk that out some other time. Oh, you're right in a way. Being is more important than doing. Many doers are just empty husks. You can see it in their eyes. There's no real person there, or only a frightened little boy. But that's not the point.

'What is?'

'I can't see you—I can't see anyone I know—just deciding that Hughes had to die. On the other hand I can see a number of people who would want to kill him for good reason. But I can't see the person who did it having any reason to.'

'Hold up,' said Irwin, suddenly solemn. 'You're not accusing me.'

'No, no, no. I'm sorry if it sounded like that. I was just wondering if you would confirm that London would be the place to get the weapon. But it leaves me with motive. There's none that I *know* of.'

'That's maybe an important qualification. How much do you know?'

Williams smiled and got to his feet.

'Look,' he said. 'Thanks for your time. It has helped. And thank you also for that promise to keep everything secret.'

Irwin smiled more broadly. 'I won't say anything.'

'It's just that it is a worry. You don't mind ministers having worries, do you?'

'No, I don't mind. What I do mind is them having doubts about God and all sorts of things and still demanding that people pay attention to them. You're not a "conjuring-tricks-with-bones" man, are you?'

'No.'

'Good. In that case I might come to a service or two. But if you were one of those . . .' Irwin turned and spat into the fire.

'You don't approve of some of my colleagues?'

'No. If they were honest, believing what they say they do, they would be in another job.'

'Perhaps they are unemployable,' said Williams smoothly.

Irwin began to laugh, and laughing, choked. He thumped himself on the chest, and Williams banged him on the back. The fit passed.

'Thanks,' said Irwin.

'Well, I had better be going. I'll hope to see you soon at church,' said Williams, turning towards the door.

'Ah! There you are. Typical minister. Get a promise to come to the service and you run out of the house.'

Williams shook his head. 'Not at all. That was just a coincidence. It is time that I was going. It's better to go before you fetch my coat for me unasked. I'll be back, and we would like you to come back to the manse. I don't suppose you are a model railway man?'

'No, I'm not. But how did you suppose that?'

Williams gestured to the room. 'You've been in now for some three months, and there are no models on show, nor any railway pictures.'

Irwin looked round at the room.

'Maybe I keep them all locked up.'

'No,' said Williams. 'If you were a model man there

would be at least one model on the bookcase, and probably
a shelf of railway books below it.'

Irwin clapped him on the back. 'You're all right, Minister,' he said as he showed him out. 'But I hope you'll let me
know when there is a story I can tell.'

'Yes, I will. It's a matter now of the motive.'

Irwin smiled again. 'You're doing this the wrong way
round, you know. Motive first, opportunity later. That
would be the book way to go.'

'Perhaps.'

'Try your subconscious,' said Irwin seriously.

Williams nodded.

'Thanks,' he said, waving as he went down the path.

Irwin watched him drive off. Then he looked around at
what he could see of the village. He thought of the welcome
that Williams was doubtless going back to. He remembered
that pleasant evening he had when he had visited the
Williams's, and the fun Williams clearly had with his kids.

He shivered, and went back inside.

He put the photos face down on top of the sideboard, and
opened the wine-cabinet. There was some whisky left.

Williams was turning into his own drive, when he finally
changed his mind. He stopped, reversed and went back
through the village to another house. It was starting to rain
as he got out of his car, and he hunched himself against the
wind as he waited for an answer to his ring.

The door was opened by a large burly figure.

'Colin,' said Williams. 'I'm sorry to bother you, but I
was passing and just wondered if you could help me with
something.'

'Surely. Surely, Minister. Come on in. How can I help
you. Do you want some more lessons in shooting?' Marsh
smiled broadly.

'Well, in a way that's true,' said Williams as he was
ushered into the front room.

'May,' called Marsh. 'Some tea for the minister.'
Then the two settled into a technical discussion.

In bed that night Williams lay and looked at the ceiling, his
mind whirling. He heard Jenny go to the toilet. He turned
over and felt for the small radio on the bedside table.
Tucking it beneath his ear, he turned it to the late News,
and then searched for the American Forces Network. He
got the third quarter of one of the pre-season football games,
and listened contentedly until it was over and Dallas had
won. But even that did not help. He turned over again. And
again.

'What's ado?' It was Ann.
'Nothing.'
'Must be something. You're not often awake at this time.'
'I suppose there's just a lot to think about.'
'Were you and Irwin talking about the Hughes business?'
'Some.'
'What does he think?'
'I don't know. I'm just afraid it is someone we know.'
'Oh, Ted.' Ann turned and cradled his head in her arms.
Like that, they fell asleep.

NINE: OCTOBER

1

Williams took out his double A4 sheet of paper again from the depths of his drawer. He spread it out in front of him and once more traced the red line, making one or two corrections and additions to the schema.

He sighed deeply, got up and crossed to the window. Away to the west he could see the beginnings of Carnloch valley leading to the Devil's Gate and the Grey Hill. Behind that, in the blue distance, he fancied that he could see the first snows of winter, but perhaps, he thought, that was just his eyes playing a trick in view of the TV forecast for the region. Still, it had been cold enough for snow the previous day when he had gone away up there.

He went over to the mantelpiece and picked up the object he had brought back with him. He took it back to the window and looked at it, its redness discoloured with the rain and snow of a winter and the baking of a summer. Its cardboard was dried out now, and brittle-feeling under his fingers.

He heaved another sigh, squared his shoulders, went back to his desk, and balanced the cartridge case in front of him. He stared at it, then rummaged in his address book for a number, picked up the phone and dialled. He got straight through.

'Alan? Ted here. Can I see you if I drive in today? It's important.'

Later that afternoon, Williams had a long discussion with Mason.

Two days later Mason phoned him back. 'It checks,' he said. 'Come in and we'll wire you up. We think you're right. That's the best way to flush him. I've cleared it with the Boss.'

At Greyhavens Police Headquarters Williams was taken down to the Technical Equipment room. There a cheerful sergeant fitted him out with what he assured him was the 'state of the art technology'. Williams was impressed by the results of a test.

'Just don't fidget,' was the sergeant's parting shot.

2

Miss Rettie smiled at Williams as she saw him sitting in Wade's waiting-room. She waved, and went on along the corridor. Shortly afterwards Wade himself came to collect Williams.

'Well, Minister?' he said as they settled in Wade's office. 'What can I do for you? I take it this is an official visit since you've come here. Let me guess.' He pulled a notepad towards him. 'Is it about making your will?'

'No. I've already dealt with all that sort of thing. I suppose it's really a parish matter, but I thought it best to talk to you about it here.'

Wade pushed the pad away.

'Yes?'

Williams shuffled himself in his seat a little awkwardly. He was not enjoying this.

'I was thinking how good a shot you are.'

'Yes?'

'Colin Marsh tells me that it needs great skill to be accurate with balled shot.'

Wade went still. 'I don't understand,' he said.

'I was thinking,' went on Williams slowly and carefully,

looking all the time at Wade's notepad, 'that if I had been taking money from an old woman who was likely to die without heirs, I wouldn't expect the authorities to check up on the management when the estate went to them. What is it he's called? The Queen's Lord Treasurer Remembrancer?'

'The Queen's and Lord Treasurer's Remembrancer.'

'Thank you.' Williams's gesture was graceful. 'I was also thinking that if in these circumstances an heir suddenly turned up, and I had a suitable chance, I might just take a risk.'

'What are you suggesting?'

'It is interesting that both Harold Anthony and Evan Hughes were killed by balled shot. I'm told that balled shot is caused usually by damp getting in among the shot. It was commoner in the days when cartridges were made of cardboard, though now they are made of plastic. But I think that the shot that killed Anthony came from a cardboard cartridge, or a plastic one tampered with. It takes great skill to be accurate with balled shot, as I said, but you are the best shot around, and we do know that you did shoot Harold Anthony.'

Wade snorted. 'That's rubbish,' he said. 'There was always Evan Hughes around. I knew that ages ago. So, I reckon did a good number of the PenIron older folk. Did you never see that nose on Miss Anthony?'

Williams sighed. 'But at that stage Hughes had no claim.' He looked up at Wade. 'It must have been a bad shock for you when the law changed.'

'Nonsense,' said Wade. 'I'm a lawyer. I knew the law was going to change at the end of the year.'

'Did you? I wonder. That's not the sort of reply I would expect from someone who hadn't been thinking things through, you know. I didn't say what change. What change do you mean?'

Wade frowned.

Williams continued. 'Someone else tells me that that

statute was late in being published, and that most lawyers don't keep track of changes until it comes out in those unofficial publications you folk have. Again, it just might have been the case that Miss Anthony would have died before it came into force.'

'If all that were so, then presumably I would now be trying to get rid of Iris and her child.'

'That might be true, but perhaps three deaths linked that way might be a bit much. Or maybe you draw the line at killing a woman or a child. In any case, as things are, you would be well placed. You are acting for Iris Maddon, whose child will now inherit the PenIron estate. You, acting for Miss Anthony, will make it over to you acting for Iris Maddon. That might be even safer than it going to the Remembrancer.'

'That's nonsense. In any event, someone tried to kill me, if you recall. Would it not be that I'm part of that mythical target?'

'I wondered about that. I've a feeling that it was Hughes who sabotaged your car. He was so insistent to me that your shooting Harold Anthony was an accident. Maybe he found out that the law was changing and that he might have a succession right. Maybe he got the idea that the Anthony business was not an accident after all. Maybe he had been checking out his own history, and discovered that when he was born the PenGlyph estate where he worked before he came here once belonged to the Anthony family. In any event how did he come up here?'

'He was recommended to my father, by a friend of the Anthony family and . . .' Wade's voice trailed off.

'So if Hughes thought that you had deliberately shot Harold, and worked out why, he might have thought it best to get you before you got him.'

'That's nonsense. More likely that he would have black-mailed me.'

'But he was comfortably enough off for what he was

requiring. In any case, what could you afford? Maybe you convinced him it wasn't worth it. You couldn't have too much left over after your London trips.'

Wade stood up. 'I think, Mr Williams, I have given you enough of my time without charging for it.'

He came round the desk and put his hand on the door-handle. Williams stood where he was.

'I will have to consider what you have said and our future relationship,' said Wade. 'My immediate thought would be to resign as you have impugned me so thoroughly, but perhaps I should lay this matter before the Session, and it is for you to consider your position.' He opened the door with a wide sweep.

Williams stood. 'What did he look like as you came down the valley?' he asked. 'Why did he not raise his gun?'

He crossed to the door. He put his hand in his inside pocket, took out a sheet of paper and gave it to Wade as he passed. 'There's this too,' he said. 'I hope that as you think things over you will find relevant some of the things I have preached in your hearing these years we have been together.'

3

As Williams turned into the manse drive he saw another car parked beside his garage. It was Mason's. Frowning, he went indoors.

Ann met him in the hall.

'Alan's here,' she said.

'So I see.'

'He's been here at least an hour and a half.

'Has he, the devil.'

'I've put him in the lounge. Paul is using the study to do his homework and Jenny is doing hers in the kitchen with me.'

'Did he say why he was here?'

Ann looked puzzled at her husband's tone. This was an odd way to greet the unexpected arrival of a friend. 'And there's been a police car sitting out on the main road most of the day as well. It left when Alan arrived. What is going on?'

'I'm sorry, dear,' he said, and gave her a light kiss. 'There is something doing, and Alan might know something about it.'

Ann's frown deepened.

'You mean . . .' she began.

'Yes,' he said, patted her arm and went to the study door. 'Coffee shortly?' he asked in an attempt at lightness.

'Yes,' she said uncertainly, lifting a hand as if to detain him and then dropping it to her side.

Mason was standing in front of the fire, rocking backwards and forwards on the balls of his feet.

Williams smiled. 'Reminds me of that old joke. I dreamed I went to hell, but couldn't get near the fire for all the policemen.'

'Ministers,' said Mason. 'The story has to do with ministers, not policemen, and that sounds to me like a Freudian slip.'

Williams looked his question.

'Where have you been?' asked Mason. 'I've been here for a couple of hours.'

'I went for a drive, and ended up with a walk down at the beach. It was out of my hands. I've left your equipment in the car. Was the sound all right? I was worried at one point that my moving about would muck up the sound.'

Mason nodded.

Williams sat down heavily in the chair beside the fire. 'Ann says there's been a car outside much of the day. What's going on?'

'I have many, many responsibilities, including responsi-

bilities to Ann,' Mason riposted. He sat down in the other
chair and leaned back, enjoying the discomfiture which had
come on Williams. Then he leaned forward.

'Look, old friend,' he said, 'I know how well you get along
with Jane. Nothing improper about it, but you are old
friends.'

'We should be,' said Williams with a grin. 'I was going
out with her before you came into sight.'

'Well,' said Mason, 'it's just the same, though not quite
so clear. Your wife is a fine lassie, and I will not let you do
anything that might hurt her.'

'So?' said Williams with a shrug.

'So. There was just a chance that Wade would come back
here determined to blast your life the way you have most
certainly blasted his.'

Williams picked up the poker and jabbed at the logs in
the fire. Carefully he laid another couple of logs on the fire
and poked them into place. Then, ceremoniously, he laid
the poker back on the hearth.

Mason watched in silence. Then he got up and went
across to the window. The short sunset was well advanced,
with shafts of light streaming down the cleft of the Devil's
Gate. He looked at it, and then swung round.

'He ran for it. He withdrew a huge amount from his
Client's Account, and ran. We picked him up at the airport.'

Williams sighed.

'I wasn't sure he would,' went on Mason. 'Do I gather
from your comment as you went out the door that there was
something else involved?'

'I gave him a photocopy of the Carlisle car hire.'

Mason snorted, and nodded his head. 'And you talk so
glibly about "balled shot"!' He grinned. 'That must have
been devastating.'

The phone rang.

'I'll get it,' came Ann's voice.

After a pause she came into the lounge.

'It's for you,' she said to Mason.

He went out.

'Coffee now?' Ann asked Williams, studying his face.

'Yes. Yes, please,' he said somewhat distractedly.

She nearly said something, but then went out.

Williams went back to his seat and poked the fire fussily.

Mason came back.

'You were saying . . .' began Williams.

'That was Ian Crawford,' Mason said, and stopped.

Williams looked at him.

'He's confessed. You had it to a "T".'

'Can I see him? I hated having to do that to him.'

'If he wants to see you.'

There came a knock at the door. 'Can I come in?' asked Ann.

'So,' said Mason as she entered, 'I'm sure if we alter the gearing on the drive just a little we could get a deal more power from Glen Mamie.'

'You two,' said Ann as she put down the coffee. 'Grown men. Why don't you talk about more important things.'

'Tell you later,' said Williams.